No
Family
Secrets

Patsy Collins

To Amy, Carrie, Chaz, Christopher, Dale,
Daniel, Jonathan, Kiim, Lee and Suzanne

Contents

1 No Family Secrets

If anyone in our family wants to know the truth, they ask my mum. She never lies. Not ever. Not even when the truth will tear the listener's life apart.

Once, Aunty Louise asked her if the dress she was considering wearing to a family christening made her bum look fat.

Her sister, my mum, said, "No, Louise, the weight you've put on is what's making you look fat. If you want to still be alive for that child's wedding then you'd better start living more healthily."

That makes her sound cruel; she isn't. She doesn't blurt out unwelcome news or hurtful criticism giving the excuse that she's only telling the truth. She never gives her opinion unless asked. That's why I didn't want to tell her what was on my mind. She might have thought my doubts about Kevin were a request for the truth.

That made two people she hadn't told me the truth about; the man I was to marry in two weeks' time and the man she married twenty-two years before. I hadn't let her tell me about my dad.

He'd been cycling from work, but that day he didn't make it home; he was hit by a car.

"It'll be the driver's fault, not your dad's," she'd said and I knew it was true. "He's a good cyclist, Tracie, always has been. He was riding his bicycle the day we met, did I tell you that?"

She'd told me several times about how she'd had a

puncture on her own bike and my dad had helped her mend it. I let her tell me again as we sat in the hospital whilst he had an operation. She told me, again, about the cycling tour that had been their honeymoon. Then she started to tell me about the week before they were married.

"I was so stupid," she told me. "Some friends took me away to Paris for a long weekend, as my hen party, a couple of weeks before the wedding. They teased me about all the good looking French boys, saying I'd better look at them while I was still single, because soon it would be too late."

I was born the Easter after they were married and I wondered if she were about to tell me she was already carrying me when she was married. Was the hen party spoilt by her morning sickness?

"Perhaps it was just because I was so far away from your dad, or maybe I'd have had cold feet anywhere, but I suddenly began to have the most terrible doubts about getting married. Your dad in his work boots, pedalling his clapped out old Raleigh suddenly seemed very dull in comparison to the tanned French lads. They lounged outside bars, sipping coffee. They had bicycles too, but unlike your dad, they didn't bother with fluorescent bicycle clips and protective head gear. They wore stylish jackets and open-necked shirts. They weren't quiet and polite like your dad; they whistled and winked and flirted."

"Flirted, Mum?"

"Yes, like I said, I was very stupid. I had a few drinks and…"

"Mum, is Dad going to be OK?" I asked.

I was scared to hear the answer to that question, but not as scared as I was by what I thought she was about to tell me. I don't look like my dad and I don't look like my younger sisters.

"I don't know, love," she whispered. "He's healthy. The doctors are doing all they can."

From anyone else it would have been a meaningless cliché, but hearing my mum say it comforted me a little.

"And we know he would have been wearing his helmet," she added.

Of course he would. My dad was a very sensible person. He wasn't an irresponsible, yet stylish, French boy. Definitely not.

He needed twelve pints of blood and another operation, but my dad did get better. He will be walking me down the aisle in a fortnight's time with almost no trace of a limp. That's if I do get married; if I'm not making a terrible mistake.

Kevin is a lovely bloke. He's kind and thoughtful. He's sensible, reliable and practical. He's too good to be true, my friends say. Are they right?

"What is it, love?" my mum asks. "Perhaps I can help?"

She always wants to help. When Aunty Louise agreed she was right about her unhealthy life, she went with her to aerobics classes and helped her to give up smoking. A month after my mum told her she had a fat bum, Aunty Louise's high blood pressure had started to drop and her wheezy breathing was improving.

"Kevin loves you, if that's what's worrying you," my mum said and sat next to me. "He loves you as much as your dad loves me."

"Nothing's worrying me, I'm fine."

"You can't lie to me; we're too much alike."

She was right. It was the time for the truth.

"But do I love him? And what about you and Dad… and the French boys?"

She squeezed my hand. "Yes, I do love your dad. I'll tell you a secret, I loved him from the moment I first saw him fishing on the riverbank. I waved to him every Saturday as I cycled past. He always waved back, but never spoke."

"Until you had a puncture? Lucky thing you did."

"Luck had nothing to do with it. I let it down myself."

"Mum!"

"It's all right, Tracie. I've told him the truth now and he's forgiven me."

"Just about the tyre?"

"Yes. He would probably forgive me about the French boy too, but I never told him. It's the only time I haven't been completely honest with him. I vowed that if I got away with it I'd never be dishonest again."

I didn't want to ask, but I had to. "Got away with what, Mum?"

"If you can't work that out, then we're going to have to have a very embarrassing talk before your wedding night."

"You slept with him?"

"I could blame the drinks, or my pre-wedding nerves or even French charm, but the simple fact is I was unfaithful to your dad. It was stupid. I wasn't even interested in the boy, but I risked my marriage for a few minutes…"

"So Dad isn't..?"

"No. He doesn't know a thing about it. I prayed I wasn't pregnant; I'd have had to tell him if I was, of course. When I realised I wasn't, I vowed never to lie again."

I hugged her. "And you never have."

"I've only told you now so that you'll understand when I tell you that I know how you're feeling. You're having doubts about your marriage to Kevin."

"Yes."

"We're very much alike, aren't we? You're the only one of my girls who looks like me. The only one who has the same silly doubts as me; the others are fair and sensible like your dad."

I nodded.

"Tracie, you love Kevin and you'll have a wonderful wedding and happy marriage."

So far, that's proven to be true. I smile and look at my own daughter as she tries on her wedding dress and attempts to hide her worried frown from me.

"It'll all be OK, love," I assure her. "If you don't believe me, just ask your gran."

2 Sick Leave

I soon realised I was expecting too much from a couple of weeks in the sun. At first, I'd enjoyed having everything done for me. I could sunbathe or join in family activities without having to rush in early to cook tea. I could watch the children pour milk onto their cereals without worrying I'd have to go out for more. I painted my toenails every day. After reading a book about obtaining a perfect body, I'd decided to start from the bottom and work up.

"Isn't it marvellous, the way they look after us, Alice?" Allan said.

I'd agreed. I was pleased to be able to use the bathroom without first picking up discarded clothing and removing hair from the plughole. I liked sitting on a chair, without also sitting on an i-Pod. To climb into bed, without first having to make it, was wonderful.

The hotel had cheerful staff to take care of everything. Whenever food was served, everyone smiled at the waitresses and thanked them. Allan praised the food, the nice presentation and the efficiency of the staff. On the odd occasion service was a little slow, he cut off the waitress's apologies.

"Don't worry about it, love; I can see you've a lot to do. It can't be easy keeping everyone happy."

He talked to me and the children throughout the meal, rather than staring at the TV. I was delighted to find my children were capable of stringing together a sentence that wasn't a demand I do something for them. Back in our room, Allan always noticed how clean and tidy it was.

That's what was wrong; the hotel had hardworking staff who deserved thanks when things went right and who received sympathy if they didn't. At home, the fairies did all the work and I occasionally ruined everyone's life by overcooking dinner or somehow preventing a grubby pair of jeans from spontaneously washing and ironing themselves.

One afternoon our room had not been cleaned. Allan didn't complain. He used a towel to wipe the sink, removing the toothpaste and soap scum himself.

"Just a quick wipe round can make all the difference," he'd grinned.

He ought to know, I've mentioned it often enough after he's shaved. He walked down to reception to request clean towels. Toby and Lisa went too. They carried the towels back, up three flights of stairs and along the corridor, before hanging them neatly in the bathroom. No moaning, no claiming it wasn't fair, no doing it so badly it was easier for me to do it than sort things out afterwards.

I felt so tired then. Soon we'd be home and the three of them would completely lose the ability to do anything for themselves. They'd forget every task they leave will be done by someone else; me.

Despite my irritation, I wasn't looking forward to going home. For me, that would mean no one cooking, cleaning, or doing anything else for me. For Toby and Lisa, it meant a return to school, but that's all the work they'd have. Clean clothes appear in wardrobes, food arrives on plates in front of them and their surroundings are always tidy, without them noticing, no matter where they are. There'll be a bigger difference for Allan; he'll no longer notice the work that's done around him. He'll notice I'm more tired and less fun than I was on holiday. What he won't do is offer to collect the groceries from the supermarket next to his office or cut the lawn whilst I soak in the bath. He won't pick up dirty laundry or encourage the kids to lend a hand.

I packed; the others sought out the maids who'd cleaned our room. Allan thanked and tipped them. When I'd pointed out they were just doing their job and any spare money could go towards getting the washing machine at home repaired he told me not to be mean.

"Work hard these girls do. Taken for granted most of the time I expect."

They thanked the waiting staff too, leaving a generous tip on our table. Allan thanked the cooks and people who manned reception.

"There's always someone available day and night, that's what I call real service."

He even tipped the boy who looked after the sunbeds and cleaned the pool.

"It's amazing how they keep everything so clean and neat. It's not just inside, but the grounds too. That's a lot of work."

"Well there are a lot of them, it's not as though one person does everything," I'd snapped.

"Of course not. That would be ridiculous."

The evening we travelled home, we stopped for a take-away. We ate that and crashed into bed. The following morning I surveyed the remains of supper. Lisa called from the top of the stairs.

"Mum, there aren't any clean towels in the bathroom."

"I put some in last night."

"They're all on the floor and still wet. That's so gross."

I went upstairs to the airing cupboard Lisa had walked past to call me, collected fresh towels for her and hung up the barely used damp ones.

Back in the kitchen, Allan was looking out the window.

"Don't leave the lawn too long; it's grown a fair bit since we've been away."

"I can see that."

"Sorry, just trying to help. I know it's much harder to do when it gets long."

His helpful advice didn't distract my attention from the heap of suitcases.

"It's going to take ages to unpack and wash all this stuff."

"Hmm. That reminds me; can you press my suit? I've got a meeting tomorrow morning."

"Don't forget my football kit," Toby added.

"Where is it?"

"In my room… somewhere."

"I'll need my pink dress for Janie's party, Mum." Lisa called.

"That's got a broken zip."

"You can fix it can't you? I've got to have that one. I look like a dork in anything else, you know I do. It's not fair."

"Is there anything else any of you want? I'm not sure I'm going to be quite busy enough today."

"Best get out the way, kids," Allan said. He ushered them out, then came back and gently rubbed my shoulders.

"Don't worry about getting our lunch, love. I'll take the kids out and we'll get something before we come back.

"Gosh thanks, that'll be a big help."

"Good, you'll get on faster without us under your feet too."

I'd made quite a bit of progress by the time they returned. My CD was switched off in the middle of a song, the TV recorder switched on, then they sat back to watch.

I was too tired to prepare a proper meal, so just baked some battered fish and oven chips. I dished up and took trays in. The only acknowledgement was from Toby, "You forgot the ketchup, Mum."

They finished eating, then placed their trays on the floor. They stepped over these to search the fridge for cans of Coke. I didn't trust myself to say anything. I didn't speak all evening, but no one noticed. Maybe that's because I was in the kitchen cleaning football boots, ironing a suit, mending a zip and preparing packed lunches.

I was almost in tears as I undressed for bed. Allan finally realised I wasn't happy.

"What's up, love? Didn't you enjoy the films? We got Pierce Brosnan on purpose, because he's your favourite."

Not wanting an argument before bed, I just told him I had a headache.

Just before Allan left for work, he mentioned he would prefer to eat at the dining table that evening.

"That way we can all talk to each other instead of staring at the TV."

He had a point of course. If I'd told him what was wrong yesterday, I would have mentioned the way they'd taken the trays of food, without seeming to notice me.

Before work, I finished ironing everyone's clothes. I cleaned and tidied the bathroom, but resolved to insist that towels were either hung up or brought down for washing. I didn't make the children's beds. If they wanted their duvets straightened, they could do it themselves. I realised my discontent was at least partly my fault as I'd let them get away with treating me like a dogsbody. It was time things changed.

As we sat together around the dining table, I sipped my drink. The others just stared at me.

"Dinner not ready yet?" Allan asked.

I leant back on my chair and looked into the kitchen.

"Yes it is, I can see it on the side."

"What's it doing there?" Toby demanded.

"Don't know," I shrugged. "Perhaps the waitress is busy. I expect someone will bring it soon."

Toby went into the kitchen, collected one plate and returned. His sister then did the same. Allan fetched the remaining food and put a plate in front of me.

"Thanks, love." I smiled at him.

Once the plates were empty, Lisa asked, "Is there any dessert?"

"Chocolate gateaux. It's in the fridge."

Lisa collected it.

"We'll need a knife to cut it," I pointed out.

Allan fetched that and the dessert bowls. I cut the cake; placing a portion into three of the bowls, as I passed one to Lisa, she moved her dirty plate to the side. Allan put mine and his own on top of Lisa's. I handed Allan his cake and put a bowl at my place. The fourth slice I put onto the gravy smeared plate that was in front of Toby.

"What you do that for?" he whined.

"It will be one less thing for you to wash up."

"Me? Lisa never washes up, why should I?"

"Because I won't be cooking any more food until there are clean plates to put it on, that's why," I screamed at him.

Allan held my wrist and asked, "What's wrong, love?"

As well as shouting, I'd been waving the cake knife

around. I sat down and took a couple of deep breaths. I wanted to say how tired I was of doing everything without any thanks; to explain I was angry they appreciated hotel staff, but not me.

"I don't think you're very well, Mum," Toby informed me.

Before I could think of a suitable reply he'd put his hand on my forehead. "You've got a temperature and a rash on your neck."

He was right; I went to bed. The following morning the children attempted to make their own breakfast. Allan called the doctor. I assured them I could be left whilst they went to school and work. I wasn't so ill I couldn't lie on the sofa with the phone close by and wait for the doctor.

When the children returned from school, I explained I had chickenpox and must rest. Allan came in to find the breakfast things still on the table, with additional debris from after school snacks.

During the next fortnight, my family learnt someone actually has to put the dirty clothes into the washing machine for them to get clean. They learnt it's quicker to hang up towels than to wash and dry them. After two loads, Allan said he'd had enough of rinsing and wringing out everything by hand and ordered a new machine.

"It's really hard work," he told me, as if that could be something I didn't know.

They learnt it takes time to prepare a meal and that after putting in that effort it's nice to be thanked.

Gradually, although my spots were still red and angry looking, I began feeling much better. I started appreciating the things Allan and the children were doing around the house.

"That was a lovely meal, Lisa, thanks."

"That's OK, Mum."

"Nearly as good as your mum's cooking," Allan said.

Lisa grinned at the compliment.

"Thank you for cutting the lawn, Toby. It looks very neat now."

"No problem. Oh wow, you've fixed the rip in my jacket, it looks great."

"Thanks for doing the shopping, Allan. I don't feel like showing my face in public yet."

"Actually I did it in my lunch break so it wasn't a problem. I hadn't thought of that before. I'll get everything except the frozen stuff in future."

"Thanks, it was a struggle on the bus."

My spots have faded and I've returned to work. I'm doing housework again, but not all of it. I wash clothes, but don't search the house for them. When I serve a meal, I'm thanked and often Toby or Lisa washes up. I'm not called upstairs to fetch things they've just walked past. The best bit is I don't have two weeks of this before I come home and things return to normal. I am home and things are just fine.

Well, nearly fine. There is homework abandoned on the kitchen table, coffee mugs discarded in the living room and a grimy ring round the bath. I think I'd better sit down. I'm sure I can feel a bout of flu coming on.

3 The Ice Cream Man

I always thought of Uncle Giorgio as the ice cream man. I suppose I still do, even though, now that I'm twelve, I know the truth. When he came to visit me, he always brought presents and paid for treats. He'd take me to the zoo, a theme park, the pictures, anywhere I liked. Almost every time I saw him, he bought me an ice cream. It might be a tub with coloured sprinkles, or a cornet topped with a Flake, occasionally we'd go to a restaurant and have huge Knickerbocker Glories or hot fudge sundaes. Sometimes Mummy came on these outings. Daddy never did.

Mummy and I didn't talk much about the ice cream man, just things like, "Go and put on a pretty dress, your uncle Giorgio will be here soon, Anne."

That was another reason for thinking of him as the ice cream man. Mummy would make sure I was always prettily dressed, frilly pastel dresses in ice cream colours, ribbons in my hair, reminding me of swirls of cream decorating my favourite desserts. We never mentioned Uncle Giorgio when Daddy was there. I didn't think Daddy liked him.

I knew that I'd been adopted and I began to daydream that the ice cream man was really my father. Daddy was strict. "Eat your vegetables or there'll be no pudding for you, Anne," he'd say. He didn't let me get the bus home from friends' houses or the pictures. He always insisted on picking me up, in his bright orange car. He wouldn't let me go out until I'd done all my homework, even if it wasn't due in for days.

The ice cream man was different. We always went

wherever I wanted to go. He always had plenty of time for me. We never had to queue for hours in the bank or post office on the way. If I wanted to go on rides or have chips, he didn't remind me about the price of the new trainers I wanted. To me he seemed rich and I imagined a life of luxury was waiting for me. It was all just a childish fancy; I didn't really want to leave Mummy and Daddy.

One day at school, I fell and smashed my leg. It really hurt. A teacher fetched Mummy, who came to the hospital with me. I had to have an operation. Mummy kissed me beforehand and was waiting for me when I came round afterwards. Daddy was at work.

I cried. I didn't like being in hospital, I was sick, my leg hurt and I just wanted to go home. A doctor came and told me my leg would get better. He showed me an X-ray of it before he mended it and explained I had to rest it. He said I was very brave, which made me proud.

There were other children in the hospital, some were ill and some, like me had suffered accidents. I had the biggest plaster cast in the whole ward. One boy who had been there three days went home. I felt better then. I had been there one day already, perhaps I could go home very soon?

The ice cream man came to see me that afternoon. He brought flowers and books and chocolates (proper ones in a box with a bow) and a big basket of fruit. He was telling me about all the wonderful places he would soon take me, when Daddy arrived.

Uncle Giorgio said, "I'll leave you with your father then."

They didn't talk to each other. Daddy came and stood next to me. He looked like he wanted to hug me, but he didn't touch me. He blew his nose a bit, and I thought he'd got something in his eye.

"I'm OK except for my leg, Daddy."

He did hug me then. "I didn't bring you a present, love. I came straight from work as soon as I heard."

"That doesn't matter, I'm glad you're here. I thought I'd have to wait ages to see you."

He blew his nose again, and I realised he was crying.

I did have to stay a bit longer than three days, but it wasn't too bad once I stopped feeling sick. Ever so many people came to see me, and lots of them brought presents and cards. All my friends from school came, and some teachers. Mummy was there quite a lot. Uncle Giorgio came every afternoon and Daddy came every evening. The ice cream man came to visit on my last day. He was still there when Daddy came to take me home. Daddy started collecting up all my presents as soon as he'd hugged me.

"Shall I carry some of these to your car?" Uncle Giorgio asked him.

"Thank you," Daddy said.

They put some of my things in the car. Daddy helped me get in. He had to move the seat right back because I couldn't bend my leg. Uncle Giorgio collected the rest of my gifts and cards. We were just about to drive away when Daddy wound down the window.

"You can come to the house tomorrow, if you like," he said.

"I would be delighted," Uncle Giorgio said.

Then we went home. Mummy made a special tea for me, and some of my friends came to see me. I soon felt tired and went to bed.

The next day my parents said they wanted to talk to me about something important.

"When we told you that we adopted you, we said we didn't know anything about you before you were ours. That was true then, but we did find things out afterwards," Mummy said.

"Sorry we didn't tell you everything, we thought you might be upset and confused," Daddy added.

"But I'm more grown-up now, so you'll tell me?"

Mummy just nodded and held my hand.

"Your rea… your first parents died," Daddy told me. "There didn't seem to be any other family, so we were lucky and got to keep you. Later, the father of your first dad found out about you. He had lost contact with his son, and hadn't known you existed, until after the adoption. We agreed that he could see you sometimes. Your mum wanted you to know about him, but I didn't. I was scared he might try and take you away, or that you'd love him more than me."

"But that's silly, I could never love anyone more than you and Mummy."

He hugged me tight.

"I would like a granddad though, so will I be able to meet him?"

When I'd said that, Mummy and Daddy just looked at each other. Then the doorbell rang, and Mummy let in the ice cream man. Then I realised.

"Hello, Granddad," I said. Then I wished I hadn't because they all started crying.

The ice cream man touched Daddy's arm, "Thank you."

A few days later, we went to the beach for the day. As Daddy carried me right into the sea, Mummy held carrier bags over my leg to keep the cast dry. I dangled my good leg, so that my foot was in the water. Granddad bought us an ice cream each and we ate them on the beach.

4 Cold Feet

Cold feet, that's what every one says I have. Every bride suffers them in the build up to her big day. It's just the thought of standing before the altar in a beautiful dress and proclaiming your love before God for all to hear. That is a scary thought, especially for me as I am shy and softly spoken. He will hear me though and that's what matters. I suppose my friends are right; it's natural to be nervous. What if they're wrong though? How do I know if I'm doing the right thing?

Some of my friends think I should listen to the doubts. They think I could never be happy, married, but having to share my love. He has other wives and many dependent children, but that doesn't mean he doesn't love me too. They can't understand why I would choose a life so different from theirs. They want me to be happy but not to be so far removed from their lives.

I asked Mother for guidance.

"Look into your heart, daughter. Think of nothing but him and you will know."

I do think of him all the time, but still I have doubts. "Did you never have misgivings, regrets?" I ask.

"I have never regretted my choice. Some days are easier than others, as they are with all relationships. It's true that love changes over the years. I have always loved your father and he has always loved us."

I look into the evening sky for some kind of sign or reassurance to make my decision for me. I pray silently that

I am doing the right thing as I put tiny invisible stitches into the hem of my gown. As I sip some wine I hope I'm taking in answers along with the calories.

I worship him, have done so since I was a child and he first came into my life. My uncle carried out the introduction. We were at a family wedding; I was too young to understand about love and asked Uncle Jim to explain some of the things which had been said in the service. My uncle, naturally enough, didn't wish to explain too much about married life to his twelve-year-old niece. He told me not to worry as I would always be loved and that when the time was right I would know what to do. This didn't help a lot, but he then introduced me to a couple of lads from the choir who'd sung for the bride and groom. As with many choir boys their angelic looks were just for show and not entirely reflected in their personalities. Peter, the eldest was very funny and I soon forgot to be shy with him. We helped decorate the wedding car and pushed a vol-au-vent into the exhaust. We spent the rest of the reception together and swapped phone numbers.

At first it was just at weekends, when I could spare time after school and my homework was done. I fitted him in around window shopping with my mates and following my favourite bands. He was always there on the edge of my life. As I got to know him I realised he was something special. It took years, but eventually he was more than a part of my life. In a way he was my life. His family, his home could be mine if I chose him. My work, what I ate, how I dressed, even the people I mixed with; all were influenced by him. He made me happy and content in a way no one else could.

I'd had a few dates with lads from college. I liked them and had fun but even as a teenager, I knew that wasn't love. I never had flings like some of my friends. At first they thought I was boring and stuffy,

"Go on, Jen, live a little; you don't know what you're missing."

But gradually they got used to me and accepted I was different from them. Like them I wanted a gold band on my finger and eternal love and happiness. Like them I knew most lads can't promise this. Unlike them I found the one man who could make my life complete. Was it any wonder that, if there are so few good men, I would have to share the one I'd found?

I love him with all my heart, but I don't know if I can commit my life to him. He will always love me, I know. He would love me as his bride or as a friend if that was what I wanted. If I left him and came back he would forgive and welcome me. He wants me to be his, and his alone, but has made it clear he will always love the others too. He will never abandon those who love and need him. The ceremony is only a week away; I have to make up my mind quickly.

This is to be so much more than a ceremony and beautiful singing; it is a big commitment. It is more than a girl in a white dress standing in chapel promising to love her man. My name will change. I will not be able ever again to go where I like and do as I like, without first considering far more than my own desires. I will have to dress differently. I will not live among my family and friends. I shall not be completely cut off from the world, but I shall be different.

It has been a difficult decision to make. I have spoken to him every night and been completely honest regarding my doubts. When I'm talking to him I can feel how much he loves me. I love him; that has never been in doubt, but marriage? It is such a wonderful opportunity to end one life and begin another. Sounds dramatic, but for me it's true. I shall have a fresh start with a new identity. I shall have a home, a new family, love and security always. Is that what I want?

Mother told me to think of nothing but him, I followed her advice but this didn't silence my doubts. Some of my friends liked Peter; they thought he would be a far more suitable husband. I jokingly told Peter what they had said and was shocked to hear he agreed.

"I'd be glad to marry you, Jen. I didn't ask because I thought you'd made your decision."

"I thought so too."

"I can't help you decide, but if it turns out to be more than cold feet, just let me know."

I thanked him, but in truth his words had confused rather than comforted me.

I then thought of my uncle, it was he who had introduced us. I knew Uncle Jim would remember the little girl who was confused about love. He helped me then and would try again.

"Don't think of him at all. Imagine life without him; imagine days and nights without him by your side."

"No, Uncle; no I can't. My life without him would be empty, pointless."

"It's you, little Jenny, who must answer your questions. Sounds like you just did."

Uncle Jim was right of course. That's why I'm standing here in my white dress. I proclaim my love before God for all to hear. The convent chapel is filled with beautiful hymns as I join my new sisters in Christ to serve our Lord Jesus forever.

5 Mother

"You can't go. Please, I can't lose you," Sue pleads.

"Don't be ridiculous. I'll be back in three days."

"Jamie will be five on Saturday, he needs a father."

"And I'll be back on Thursday, Sue."

She turns away from him so he can't see the tears.

"Come on, love, what's all this about? It's just a routine trip, about the twentieth this year. You've never minded before."

"It's not the trip, Chris. It's the flight. Please, you can't get on that flight."

"Why not?"

"Something bad will happen. I know it will."

"You know?"

"Mother told me. She said you mustn't."

"Your crazy old mother! I'm sick of this. I thought you'd got over all that rubbish. She's never been anything more than an irrational old bat, scaring gullible people half to death with her prophesies of doom."

"She loves us and is just trying to protect us. And she has been right, you know she has."

"Coincidence."

"You didn't say that after the fire."

"It was an emotional time; we had to find another hall for the reception just days before the wedding. Anyway, we were in love and just about to get married. I was hardly going to tell your mother she was an old witch was I?"

"And now you don't love me so it doesn't matter what you say or how I feel."

"Of course I love you. Don't turn this around."

"I love you too, that's why I don't want you to go."

"Because of something the Old Crone told you?"

She smiles at the use of their nickname for her mother.

"Do you remember why you called her that?"

"Yeah it's from when we watched that Robin Hood film."

"We took Ricky with us didn't we?"

"Yeah, your mother warned us not to leave him with the baby sitter."

"Who turned out to be a bad tempered drunk. So she was right?"

"That's not second sight, Sue. It just shows remarkable judgement of character."

"She told me the first time she met you that you were a good, sensible man who would always put his family first."

"Which is why I don't listen to superstitious mumbo jumbo, and work hard at my job to earn enough money to provide a good life for us all. Am I a bad husband then?"

"Now who's turning things around?" She picks up his suitcase, spilling the contents onto the carpet.

"Look, love, please don't let us argue about this. You know I have to go. This deal is critical to the company."

"And the company's future is more important than your family's?"

"Of course not. You know I love you and the kids."

"Then don't get on that flight. Please, just don't go."

"You know I have to." He gently pushes past her and goes into the bathroom to collect his toiletries.

"Mother is right I know she is," Sue stubbornly insists to his back.

"You and your bloody mother." He hurls the bottle of aftershave into the sink. The explosive crash of glass onto china almost drowns out his angry curse. The cologne stings their eyes. His are almost as red as hers now.

"That does it. I'm fed up with your flaming mother running my life. She controlled you until I got you to see sense. You couldn't drink a cup of tea without worrying what the leaves would say. I got you to change to teabags and nothing bad happened. You wouldn't look towards the sky in case the clouds showed some terrible fate, so I bought you a book about the weather and now you can hold your head up. On Friday the thirteenth you wouldn't get out of bed. You had to when I booked that carpet fitter and nothing bad happened did it? And nothing bad will happen when I get on that plane. Now you can help me to finish my packing or leave me in peace. Which is it to be?"

Silently she picks up his suitcase and the spilt contents. She refolds things neatly. When it's all carefully packed she goes to her dressing table and detaches a silver charm from the bracelet her mother gave her. She takes her husband's hand and places the symbol of St Christopher in his palm before curling his fingers around it. He looks at it, smiles, then without a word places it into his breast pocket.

Sue waves her husband goodbye as cheerfully as she can, but as she closes her front door she sinks down behind it sobbing. She cries until exhausted, then just sits, staring at the skirting board.

She remains crouched uncomfortably on the floor until early evening, eventually roused by the telephone. Her youngest son asks if he may spend the night at his friend's.

"Of course you can, love, when will you be back?"

"Tomorrow afternoon sometime. Dad get away OK?"

"Yes, love."

"He must be there by now."

"Yes, yes he must."

"See ya then."

"Yes bye, love." Sue checks her watch, walks into the lounge and picks up her wedding photograph. She holds it tightly against her, until the silver frame pressing into her arms becomes uncomfortable. Gently she touches the image of Chris's face then places the picture back in its position on the sideboard. Smiling at their image she shrugs her shoulders, and then begins the routine tasks that keep her home running smoothly.

She'd noticed dust trapped under the skirting board, there's broken glass to be removed from the bathroom and supper to prepare.

"Mum, where's Dad?" Ricky calls as he lets himself into the tidy little house.

"He's in Frankfurt. He'll be back on Thursday, but you know his travel arrangements as well as I. You helped him look on the internet for the cheapest fares."

"You've heard from him?"

"No, not yet. I'm sure he will call soon."

"When did he leave? What flight did he get?"

His uncharacteristic abruptness startles her.

"Why, what's happened? Oh, Ricky I begged him not to go. Something's happened hasn't it? Just tell me."

"Come and sit down."

"I don't want to." She snaps at her son before realising for the first time how upset he is. "Come on, darling, we'll both sit down and you can explain what's happened."

They sit close together on the sofa. Sue can feel her son's thigh trembling against her own. She senses he is trying to keep calm in order to speak clearly.

"There's been an accident. I heard it on the radio. A plane crash. No survivors." His voice is so weak she has to sit with her head touching his to hear him. Her need to care for her son is all that enables her to keep control of her own emotions.

"The evening news will be on soon, we must watch that to find out which flight has crashed, then you can check his travel details on the computer. You are better at working that thing than I am."

Together they watch the news in silence holding hands tightly. Ricky then calls up his father's diary on the computer. She doesn't need to look for herself. Her son's tears on the keyboard tell her all she needs to know.

"Maybe he missed the flight," she suggests.

"He'd be back home by now if that was true."

She can barely understand his words, drowned as they are in his tears.

"Mum."

The word is no more than a gulp of despair. Ricky, still on his father's chair, takes hold of his mother, burying his head against her stomach. She rests her hand on his heaving back.

"Ricky, listen. I don't believe he's dead. I'm sure I would know. Grandma would have told me."

"Grandma! I don't understand. What does she have to do with this?"

"Oh darling, it's hard to explain. Before your father left I was terrified that something bad would happen. Your grandma told me to stop him going."

"Yes, you said you told him not to go. But this doesn't

help. Grandma didn't help. He still went didn't he?"

"Yes, but your grandma's not here now is she?"

"No, of course not."

Ricky scans through information on the computer. Sue knows he's barely listening to her, all his concentration is taken up with searching for anything that might indicate his father wasn't actually on that particular flight.

"She wouldn't leave me if your dad had just died. She must have stopped it happening somehow."

"Mum, you're not talking sense. How could Grandma stop a plane crash? I mean she didn't, the plane has crashed, we saw it on the news."

Mother and son stop talking. Sue unable to explain to him her sense of calm and belief that all will be well. Ricky in turn still searching the computer files.

"There's an e-mail shall I read it?"

"It will probably be for your father."

"No he sent it. It's for you. He must have sent it from the airport before he left." The message is opened; it reads 'The Old Crone got to me direct. Will call about eight your time.'

"What's the time?" Sue asks.

"Three minutes past."

As he replies the phone rings. Sue answers but when Chris speaks she sags back onto the sofa unable to speak. Ricky takes the phone from her and switches it to loudspeaker.

Chris's voice fills the room; a tinny echo of the man.

"I thought I heard someone call out my name as I was waiting to check-in. I looked round and there was a woman looking rather like your mother staring straight at me and shaking her head. It shook me up so much I asked if there was space on the later flight. There'd been a cancellation shortly before. It seemed like fate, so I changed flights. But look, nothing happened so I know I shouldn't say it but, told you so."

Ricky explains about the crash.

"God I didn't know. Thank your mother for me."

"Mum's right here, Dad."

"I know, son. She knows what I mean."

"We'll all thank her when you get back," Sue said.

On the Friday, the family go together to visit the lady who so many times had issued warnings in order to protect those she loved. On the way the yellow freesias they have brought fill the little car with their fragrance.

"Ricky, Jamie, some special people are like these flowers. When we take them to your grandma, the flowers themselves will be gone but the scent will linger in the car. Grandma is like that; she is always with us, watching over us."

They stand before her, Chris's arms wrapped around both his wife and younger son. Ricky has hold of his mother's hand. Chris clears his throat and, clearly embarrassed, apologises to his mother-in-law.

"Mum, I'm sorry I never really believed in your power. I always thought you were a bit batty. I thought you were just playing on your gypsy background. You know, just trying to get a bit of attention. If I'm honest I didn't want to believe in it. It scared me to think I was marrying into a family of psychics. I know better now. Thank you."

"Thank you, Mum," Sue says.

"Yeah, thanks, Gran," adds Ricky.

Slowly, Chris kneels and places the flowers on his mother-in-law's grave.

6 Drawing Conclusions

Keeping tight hold of her granddaughter's hand, Jean stepped onto the bus. She had to let go to pay the driver and put the tickets into her bag.

"Don't run, Millie. Wait for me."

It was too late; Millie had already selected a seat. Jean joined her, wishing Millie hadn't sat so close to the big ugly man in the leather waistcoat. As Jean looked at the back of his shaved head and tattooed arms, she wondered why he was on a bus at all. Probably caught drink driving and lost his licence, she guessed.

Jean looked through the window, searching for interesting things to show Millie.

"Look at that dog, Millie. He looks just like Benjy, from next door."

"I like dogs, Granny. Can we take Benjy for a walk?"

What a good idea. It was hard work keeping Millie occupied.

"I can't promise, Millie, because he's not my dog, but Mr and Mrs Singh might let us help walk him. We'll ask when we get home."

"When will that be, Granny?"

"Later on, Millie. First we have to buy things you'll like to eat, then I thought we could go to the park."

"A park? Yes please. Are there swings? I like swings."

"Yes, swings and a slide and roundabout and a pond."

"Can I go on the swings?"

"Yes, love."

"Are there ducks on the pond?"

"Yes. Would you like to feed them?"

"Yes please. What shall we feed them?"

"Bread."

"Have you got any in your handbag?"

"No, Millie. We'll buy it."

"Where from?"

Jean sighed; it was going to be a long fortnight.

"From the supermarket. I think we should write a shopping list. Would you help me with that?"

"OK, Granny. I'm good at writing, Mummy said so. Can we write to Mummy and Daddy?"

"Yes, later." Jean handed Millie a pen, before rummaging through her bag for something the child could write on.

"Later on after we've feeded the ducks and gone on the swings and taken Benjy for a walk?"

"Yes, I suppose… Oh, Millicent, don't do that!"

"Do what, Granny?"

"Don't draw on your arm."

"Why not, Granny? That man's got drawings all over him."

"Shh."

He turned and smiled at them. He needn't think a charming smile would get around her. It had been a leather-clad, tattooed man with a charming smile, who'd whisked her daughter away. Jean had made a mistake then; she wouldn't do it again.

"But, he has, Granny. Look."

"Don't point, it's naughty."

"Why is it?"

Jean didn't have a chance to answer. She was almost jolted out of her seat as the bus swerved across the road. Millie cried out. Jean tried to reassure her everything was all right. There was another lurch. The bus swerved again and stopped abruptly. Both Millie and Jean were thrown off the seat. Millie's cry of alarm turned to screams. The girl was on the floor of the bus. Her arm was horribly twisted, her hand still grasping the top of the seat.

Gently, Jean coaxed her to relax her fingers. As Millie's arm slid down against her body, the girl fainted. Her skin was pale and sweaty. The arm was broken.

"Help her," Jean called. She looked toward the driver's seat. The door to his compartment was open. The driver lay on the floor. The tattooed man was leaning over him, hitting him in the chest.

Jean felt as though she too had been punched in the chest. How could she carry poor Millie to safety without the man attacking them too? She wasn't sure they'd be any safer staying where they were. The man must be mentally ill, or on drugs to attack the driver like that. He could turn on them at any minute.

A terrible metallic banging sound started and the bus began to shudder. Another lunatic was trying to force his way in. It was only a moment before he wrenched the doors open. Jean leant over Millie, hoping to protect the child with her own body.

"What on earth happened?" the new man demanded.

Jean looked up. The newcomer was dressed in uniform. One of those community support workers; they were saved.

"Driver had a heart attack, I think," the tattooed man explained. "The bus swerved across the road. I managed to drag him out his seat and stop the bus before we hit anyone. I hope I haven't injured him, but there wasn't time to be gentle. I don't suppose it matters. He's not breathing, I've tried to revive him, but…"

"I'll carry on. You call an ambulance."

The uniformed man started pumping the driver's chest.

"Ambulance please," the tattooed man spoke into his mobile, giving their location. "I'm on the bus. The driver isn't breathing, he's receiving CPR. There's a child injured too, I think."

The tattooed man approached Jean. "Is she badly hurt?" he asked.

"Her arm is broken."

"Are you OK?"

Jean nodded.

The tattooed man returned to the bus driver and assisted the resuscitation efforts. An ambulance arrived, quickly followed by a second and a police car. The bus driver was taken away and a stretcher brought for Millie.

Jean held her granddaughter's good hand during the journey and spoke soothing words. Millie came round, but was quiet and pale.

"Sorry I was naughty, Granny."

"Shh, don't worry about that now."

At the hospital, the girl's arm was X-rayed. Jean was asked so many questions and given so many forms, she felt she was losing track of events. All she understood was that, with the girl's parents on holiday, Millie was undergoing an operation and Jean was in a waiting room with no idea of what she should do next. Contacting her daughter would be difficult and she wasn't sure she should try. By the time she and Simon had flown back, Millie would be out of hospital.

Why worry them? Millie would need night clothes and her teddy. Jean didn't want to leave the hospital until she'd spoken to Millie and assured her she would come back. She didn't know how she would get home. There might be a bus into town, she supposed.

"Are you OK?" a man asked.

She looked up, it was the tattooed man.

"Yes, thank you. I am unhurt. My granddaughter is being operated on. Someone will be here any minute to tell me how she's getting on."

"I hope she's going to be OK. Millie, I think you called her?"

He sat next to her. Jean remembered he'd called the ambulance. Without his help, Millie would have waited longer for treatment. Wasn't it him who stopped the bus? She shook her head to try to clear it; really, she couldn't remember what had happened.

"What happened to the driver?" she asked.

"They got him breathing again in the ambulance, they're operating now."

At the mention of an operation, Jean stopped listening. Her thoughts concentrated on poor Millie and the surgery she was receiving.

"Milk and sugar?" the man was asking.

She stared.

He touched her arm. "Little Millie will be all right. Kids are resilient. I bet she's had lots of knocks and bruises and bounced back?"

"I don't know, I've not seen much of her. My daughter moved away and ..." Jean trailed off as she began to cry.

"I'll get that tea, shall I?"

"Tea? Oh, yes. Thank you."

"Milk and sugar?"

Jean nodded and he left. She needed the tea. It was kind of him to offer to fetch it. She'd done it again, judged someone by appearances. Perhaps paying for their teas would ease her conscience. She'd get the money ready.

"There you go," he was back and handing her a plastic cup.

"How much do I owe you?" Jean waved her purse at him.

"Nothing." He sounded very definite about it.

They sipped their drinks.

"I think I might know Millie's parents."

"I hardly think so. My daughter went to St Jude's and now lives some distance away."

"Lorraine and Si, right?"

"Well…"

"I went to college with Si. We exchange Christmas and birthday cards, that sort of thing. He sent me a picture of Millie when she was tiny. Proper proud he was. Tell him Kev Pearson says 'hello' would you?"

Before Jean could reply, a nurse came in.

"Mrs Wilkinson?"

Jean looked up.

"Millie is in the recovery room now. Her arm has been set and she's doing fine. You'll be able to see her soon."

"Thank you, nurse."

"Nurse?" the man asked. "Is there any news of the bus driver?"

"Are you family?"

"No, it was me who, er who called the ambulance."

"You're the man from the bus?"

"Hmm."

"Thanks to you, he's now stable. It's early days, but he stands a good chance." She turned to Jean. "He's a real hero isn't he?"

"The bus driver?"

"No, no. This chap. It wasn't just the driver he saved. His quick thinking stopped your bus from crashing into a car coming the other way. Reckon he saved that family too, not to mention what would've happened to you and Millie if the bus had tipped over."

"Oh."

When the nurse had left, Jean looked down at the purse still in her hands and allowed it to flip open. Inside were two of her precious photographs of Millie.

"You were wrong. You said I didn't owe you anything, but I do. I owe you everything."

"No, don't be daft. I just did what anyone would do."

Jean looked down at the pictures; photographs that Simon had sent. She remembered his first brief note. 'I'm sorry the two of us can't get along. I hope that needn't deprive Millie of a grandmother, nor you of a grandchild.' A photo had been enclosed. She'd realised then that she had been wrong about Simon. She'd rung and asked Lorraine to visit and bring Millie to see her.

"Do you mean just me, or my family too?" Lorraine had asked.

"Of course, I'd like to see my granddaughter."

"I meant Si."

The call had ended abruptly, before Jean could explain her feelings. She'd held the silent receiver in her hand and stared at the photo. Despite her dislike of Simon, she knew he was right. Her stubbornness was only punishing herself and Millie. She'd called back and Simon had answered. Jean had taken a deep breath and then invited them all to visit.

"Thank you," Simon had said. "We'd love to." He lowered his voice. "I reckon the two of us could learn to get along for Lorraine and Millie's sakes."

"I'm sure I can behave in a civilised manner."

When she'd seen the fake tattoos he'd bought Millie, she'd struggled to keep that promise, but she'd managed. To be fair, Simon had been extremely polite and there was no doubting his devotion to Millie. Over several visits, Jean had found the courage to admit she'd been mistaken about Simon. She was delighted to be part of a family again.

A few weeks ago, Lorraine had called.

"Mum, Si suggested taking me on holiday; we wondered if you'd like to have Millie to stay?"

Of course, Jean was happy to agree.

"Mrs Wilkinson?"

Jean looked up. The tattooed man looked concerned.

"Are you all right? I was just asking if you'd like a lift back to the village? You'll need things for Millie if she stays in."

"But you were on the bus …?"

"I was on my way to collect my car. I'll get a bus into town now and come and pick you up. Hopefully you'll have seen Millie by then, but if not, I'll wait."

Jean did see Millie and explained she would be going for just a little while, to fetch teddy, and then she'd be back. The hospital arranged for her to stay in the next bed.

The tattooed man came back as promised.

"Thank you. I'm sorry, I've forgotten your name."

"I'm not surprised with all that's happened. It's Kevin."

"Kevin, you asked me if I was all right. I lied to you. I said I was. I wasn't. I was all wrong. About you; and about Simon."

"Si? Oh, what's wrong with him?"

"Nothing. Well, nothing except that he'll probably want to draw a fake tattoo on Millie's cast…"

7 Thinking Things Through

Marion admired the art deco inspired picture frame she'd made. She was very proud of it. Almost exactly a year ago, she'd seen one on television and begun dreaming of creating something as beautiful. Marion placed the frame onto the mantelpiece, next to the brass casket of ashes. It reminded Marion of the events that caused her return to jewellery design.

She'd sighed as the expert on the television examined a beautifully enamelled art deco picture frame.

"What's up with you now?" Cliff had asked.

"That frame is lovely; I wish I could produce something like it."

"Well you shouldn't have given up that jewellery design course. Don't think things through, that's your trouble."

Marion bit her lip. She had given up the course when she married Cliff. In order to afford a mortgage they'd both had to work. Cliff had told her to think about the money they'd waste in rent if she stayed on at college. She knew better than to remind him, it was no use arguing with Cliff. Instead, she rang South Downs College and discovered they held Jewellery and Metalwork design courses on Wednesday evenings. They had space available. She'd have plenty of time to cook Cliff's dinner before she made the short drive to the college and would almost be back again before he was wanting a cup of tea. Marion promised to let them know.

A few days later over supper she'd told Cliff, "I've been thinking about what you said and you were right."

"Of course I was."

Cliff continued to eat for a few minutes before asking, "What was I right about this time?"

"About how I should continue to study design."

"Oh, yes. Well actually I…"

"I can't give up work of course."

"Ah, so you do think sometimes then?"

"Yes, that's why I've booked an evening course."

"I bet that's expensive."

"I'll pay with the money my parents gave me for Christmas."

"Oh, all right then."

"Good, I start next Tuesday."

Cliff put down his fork.

"Tuesday? Did you say Tuesday?"

"Yes."

"But Marion, you know that's the night the boys come round to play cards. Who's going to make our snacks and keep the drinks flowing if you're not here? You don't think things through at all do you?"

"I'm sorry, Cliff," she said. "That's the only night the course is on at Highbury College."

"Highbury? That's miles away. You should have booked with South Downs, that's nearer."

"I suppose it is, but…"

"You didn't think it through, I know."

Marion enjoyed the freedom of her classes. She was able to choose what to make and to think through her own designs and ideas without constant criticism. Her first project was a small brass box. The initial design she created was exquisite. The box she made was not quite as fine and detailed as her artwork, but Marion was pleased with her efforts. The engraving was less intricate, the box heavier than she originally planned, but it was still beautiful. The tiny hinges on the lid worked perfectly. The decorative catch fitted neatly into place. Once it was finished, she took it home to show Cliff. His friends admired her skill; Cliff concentrated on his hand of cards.

It was not until Friday that he picked it up from its position of pride on the mantelpiece.

"What on earth is it? It looks like a funeral casket."

"It's a trinket box," Marion told him.

"What use is that?"

"You can put things in it."

"What things, Marion?"

"I don't know, just things."

"Nothing big, it's too small. Nothing valuable, it doesn't even lock. You should have made something practical. You didn't think it through did you? This is good for nothing."

"It was just something to learn..." Marion couldn't continue her explanation.

"You did your best, I suppose. Now you do something useful and make a nice cup of tea. That'll cheer you up."

After that, Marion stopped gazing admiringly at her creation each time she went into the lounge. On Sunday she didn't realise it was no longer in place until Cliff came in from his shed.

"Here you are, Marion. I've fixed it for you," he said.

On the front of her hand-crafted, painstakingly engraved brass box, Cliff had soldered a stainless steel padlock. He had drilled a hole through the moulded catch to take the locking mechanism. The padlock was too big, too plain. It was the wrong metal, it unbalanced the design and blobs of solder now obscured the engravings.

"What have you done?"

"Put on a lock of course. Good and safe that is."

"But why?"

"I could see you were upset that your box was no use, so I fixed it for you."

"And what use is it now? I'm sure you've worked that out."

"Like you said you can put things in it," Cliff said.

"What things? Come on, what have you got that is small and valuable that you would want to keep locked up in there?"

"Er, pills? Yes, my heart pills."

"But, Cliff, we keep those in the kitchen drawer and bedside cabinet, so they're easy to get at quickly."

"Exactly. You leave them lying around all over the place. They're important you know. I need to know exactly where they are in case I need one quickly. Now I will. They'll be nice and safe locked up in your funny little box thing."

A few nights later, Marion awoke to hear a loud crash. Cliff was not in bed beside her and she wondered if he'd got up to investigate the noise. She called his name and got no response. After a moment, she pulled on her dressing gown and crept onto the landing. Cliff was lying at the bottom of the stairs. It was his fall which had woken her. She ran down to him. He was pale and clammy. It was his heart. She ran upstairs for his pills. They were gone. Of course, he'd locked them in the box. She ran down again. Her heart felt as though it was beating for the pair of them as she climbed over Cliff and went into the lounge. Marion picked up the box then went in search of the key. She found it at last but dropped it as she tried to fit it into the lock. She had no idea how long Cliff had lain unconscious before she managed to ease a pill under his tongue and call an ambulance.

After that, Marion had time to think things through. She sat for hours, staring at her brass box. Cliff had been right; it did look a bit like a casket. She carefully placed the ashes into it, locked it and threw away the key. She never again wanted a reminder of the horror of hunting for that. Her life with Cliff and all the unhappy memories were now over.

Once the paperwork and finances were sorted out, Marion returned to college as part of a day release scheme. She managed to get a job in a jewellery shop and, by working Saturdays was able to take time off in the week for her course. The first thing she made was the enamelled picture frame, inspired by the one she'd once seen on the television.

Marion placed it next to her brass box and wondered if she had a suitable photograph. It couldn't be a wedding photograph; they were already on the mantelpiece. She'd burnt them and sealed the ashes in her box after she'd visited Cliff in hospital to inform him that, after carefully thinking things through, she wanted a divorce.

8 Family Fortune

"It was underneath that bench, Mum," Peter told Angela. He pointed across the park.

"The money for all this was under a bench? You should have handed it in to the police."

"Sorry, Mum, we tried, but they said we should put it to good use."

"Who did?"

"The policemen. We didn't recognise them. Are there new people at the station, Dad?"

"No," Ray said.

"I think you'd better explain everything from the beginning," Angela said, puzzled. The family knew all Ray's colleagues at the small rural station.

"We heard you arguing," Peter began.

"We didn't like it," Mike added.

"Arguing?" asked Ray.

"You shouted at Mum when she said something about a holiday. You said you couldn't afford luxuries, and you'd like to go for the odd beer and you'd like Mum to have nice meals she hadn't got to cook," Peter told him.

"Mummy said that you worked all the hours that there were, that she never saw you and still there was not enough for the simplest of treats." Mike's voice trembled as he recalled his parents' angry words.

Angela looked at Ray, noticing that he looked as uncomfortable as she felt. It was true. They had been arguing over money. She knew he was right, the mortgage was important and also the fund for their son's education. Still she sometimes felt unappreciated; surely, it wouldn't hurt to 'waste' a few pounds on flowers or a bottle of wine for them to share. She regretted their arguments, he was only doing what he thought was right. They were both in their teens when they lost their fathers. The men had been killed trying to stop an armed robbery. Money had been short, their mothers couldn't send them to college. Ray and Angela wanted their sons to have the chance of further education. She regretted even more that the boys had heard the arguments. She and Ray had memories of happy, loving parents. Their sons deserved the same.

"We thought we'd go and sit on the bench and see if we could find out what to do," Mike said.

"What do you mean?" Angela asked.

Peter pointed to the bench across the park. "The special one. Grandma told me that when she is sad because she misses Granddad, she goes and sits on it."

"We thought it might help," his brother said.

"And when you got there you found some money?" Ray guessed.

"Not right away. We sat talking for a bit. We thought we needed to get some money, so Mum could have flowers and Dad could have beer and we could get nice things for Grandma and Nanna. We wanted you to be able to go out, see a show, have some laughs and a nice dinner."

Angela bit her lip as she heard her own words quoted. The boys had obviously heard more than one argument.

"Two policemen walked by, and the wind was blowing our hair about," Peter told them. "Then I saw the money."

"It was a twenty pound note," Mike said.

"We thought the policemen had dropped it. They said it wasn't theirs and to put it to good use," Peter continued. "We went to the shop to see if we could buy all the things you wanted. Mr Davies helped us work it all out; he's really good at sums."

"Was it a nice dinner, Mummy?" Mike asked.

"Yes, darling, very nice," Angela said, taking another swig of warm lemonade.

"Delicious," Ray confirmed, biting into the last cherry Bakewell. "Thank you for the presents too."

Earlier that day Angela and Ray had been presented with a beautifully, if not neatly, illustrated card inviting them to dinner at six o'clock. They were sent to their room to change. On their bed, they found two packages. The stiff wrapping was decorated in a similar style to the card. On one was the inscription 'To Mum, lots of Love, from Dad' on the other 'To Dad, love from Mummy'. Ray's contained a can of ginger beer; Angela's some slightly wilted carnations.

Angela, deciding to make the most of the occasion, chose a long dress and put her hair up. Ray took the hint and wore his suit. They were glad they'd made an effort when they saw the boys had removed their usual sports outfits and were dressed in proper trousers and shirts. They'd even combed their hair.

The brothers led their parents to the park, pointing out places of interest along the way. They toured the flower beds before reaching the bench purchased in memory of their fathers. On it stood a cool box, exactly like their own. So exact was the resemblance that it had the same scratch on the handle. Next to the box was the tartan rug from Ray's mum's car.

The boys spread the blanket in the sun and invited their parents to sit. They were each given a wine glass, into which was poured lemonade.

"Mr. Davies wouldn't sell us champagne."

Ray laughed as froth bubbled over his wrist. "Never mind, Peter. This is just as fizzy."

"He wouldn't let us buy your normal beer either, but said you'd like the one we got."

"And he was right."

The boys produced plates and prawn cocktail crisps.

"These are the starter." Mike tipped them out.

The second course was sausage rolls. Dessert was a selection of cakes. The brothers told their parents about the potted pansy they'd given each grandmother.

The family finished their picnic. Angela looked at the brass plaque, and read the inscription she knew by heart. 'In loving memory of, Const. W. J. Tomlins and Const. H. Walters. Killed in the line of duty. Beloved husbands and fathers.' She vowed money would never cause problems in their family again.

"There's no more money, Mum. I checked," Mike told her.

"We don't need any more," she said, hugging her sons.

As they walked away, a breeze ruffled their hair.

9 Let Me Tell You A Story

"And then the giant intergalactic snail gobbled it all up," Jane said as she spooned a small piece of broccoli into her son's mouth.

Charlie swallowed the food and asked, "Did it work, Mummy? Did his shell glow in the dark?"

"Yes! He was amazed to see that his shell did have a very faint glow."

"Wow!"

"He had the feeling that the more of the magical vegetables he ate, the brighter his shell would glow," Jane said as she spooned up some diced carrots. "So he gobbled them all up too," she added hopefully.

Her ploy worked. Charlie took the offered spoon and began eating his dinner.

Jane grinned. Since he'd begun to understand her words, she'd told stories to Charlie and encouraged him to act out the behaviour of the characters. He brushed his teeth with the magical formula that allowed humans to talk to pixies. The foaming fluid she massaged into his hair was a super-powerful invisible formula that permitted brave knights to escape from scaly fire-breathing dragons.

Feeding Charlie a healthy diet had, until now, been a struggle. Jane and Giggernamerous, her giant intergalactic snail, had at last found a way to persuade him to finish his vegetables. As he ate, she described the wonderful colours that sparkled on Giggernamorous's luminous shell and how happy he was to be beautiful.

"Thank you for tea, Mummy," Charlie said. He picked up his plate and spoon and took them to the kitchen sink.

Whatever people said about her, they couldn't criticise the way she raised her son. At least, not if they were being fair. He didn't have a father, but it wasn't her fault her fiancé had been killed, in a car crash, just weeks before the wedding. Her dad had called her horrible names when he'd discovered she was to be an unmarried mother. She shook her head to clear the unhappy memories. Her dad hadn't been kind to her when she was a child, so it had been foolish to think he'd change just because her heart was broken and her world destroyed.

Her mum had been different. She'd done all she could to support Jane through that terrible period. For the first time in her life, her mum stood up to her dad and insisted that Jane be allowed to move back into her old home and raise her son there. Her dad had been furious at first but when he realised his wife was determined he'd accepted the situation.

Jane was grateful to have a decent place to live and the financial support of her family, so tried hard to please her dad. She'd thought the task impossible but he had surprised her by seeming proud to have a grandson. He softened, but only a little. He provided Charlie with well-fitting shoes and educational toys but never hugged the lad.

Her dad repeatedly tried to criticise her treatment of Charlie. He'd overheard her talking about the brave knight putting on his armour as she encouraged Charlie to dress himself that morning.

"You're spoiling him; you have to be firm with kids. You should let me teach him a lesson, rather than all this pussy footing around trying to get him to want to do things rather than just making him do it."

On that one point, Jane would not give in to her father's

demands.

"Charlie, go downstairs and help Granny get breakfast ready, love."

When he'd gone, she turned to her father.

"No, Dad. I'm not bringing up my son to be frightened of you or anyone else."

"Frightened? What are you on about? You're bringing him up as a right mummy's boy."

"No, Dad; I'm not. He loves and trusts me and Mum, but he's got the confidence to play with the other kids at playgroup without clinging to me and I'm sure he's going to be fine when he starts school in September."

Her dad had opened his mouth to speak, but closed it again. Perhaps he'd recognised his own stubbornness looking out of his daughter's eyes? He'd left the room and hadn't spoken to her since.

He came into the kitchen in time to see Charlie help with the washing-up as Jane told him about miners panning for gold in the river.

"Mummy, can we do writing next?"

"Yes, love. What shall we write about?"

"Writing, did you say?" her dad interrupted.

Why was he feigning interest? Jane intended to ignore his remark, but Charlie had other ideas.

"Yes, Granddad. Mummy is teaching me to do writing, just like wizards do to write their spells. Shall I show you?"

Jane watched as her dad produced paper and a pencil and stood over Charlie as he began to draw.

"First, I do a magic star." Charlie created a spiky shape. "That makes the spell and then I write in people and it does magic and makes them happy and lucky."

In wobbly letters, Charlie wrote his own name. "That's me and this is Mummy." He wrote 'mummmy' and then, 'grannny' and 'granddad'. "That's you and Granny."

"You are a very clever boy, Charlie," Jane's dad said. "Your mum has taught you very well. You're lucky too, I hope you know that?"

"Yes, Granddad. Why?"

"Because of the lovely stories your mummy tells you. When I was a little boy, no one told me stories and when your mummy was little, she wasn't told many stories either."

"Don't worry, Granddad; I'll tell you and Mummy a story. You need to get your hairbrushes though, because it's about goats with magic fur and a great big enormous troll."

10 Going Down

As instructed Cindy scanned the crowd, looking for those who stood out whilst taking care not to draw attention to herself. Her gaze followed the guy in a bulky red jacket and snug fitting blue jeans as he rode the up escalator. He wasn't a potential target, but didn't look like a threat either. Just a normal guy; the type she wanted and could never have. While she came under the protection of her brother Bryan, Cindy couldn't have anything normal, not a man or job or life. She didn't even have hope.

She had tried. Twice she took shop jobs, but Bryan turned up on every shift.

"Hello, Cupcake," he'd say. "I just came to see how my little sister is coping without me to look after her."

Sometimes he took her out at lunchtimes, just so he could enter and leave the shop twice. Always he took away as much as he could carry and her hopes of staying employed. No other work was available to her; school had been difficult. She'd often been tired after a night acting lookout or crawling in through bathroom windows, creeping around dark houses and unbolting strange doors. The library wouldn't lend her books because she couldn't return the ones Bryan took away and sold. Once she wrote about what she'd done in the holidays, but her brother saw it before she handed it in. He saw to her hand then and she couldn't write anything for six weeks.

"What you mooning about for?" Bryan asked, calling her away from the past and the man on the escalator. His sharp tone matched his smart suit. "You forgotten our plan?"

His plan, he meant. It never occurred to him that she could have a thought in her head except to do what he told her.

"No, Bryan. I haven't forgotten. We go into the jeweller's behind Fingers and Baz. Baz is going to act shifty so they're going to be watching him. We'll ask to look at pricey engagement rings. I pick the flashiest and ask to try it on. We act like we're in love."

Acting was something Cindy was good at, she demonstrated by placing a hand on Bryan's arm and smiling confidently up at him. "I pretend to sweet-talk you and flash them my assets. Then, when I'm sure that Baz and I have everyone's attention, I'll faint. While you and they fuss over me, Fingers grabs the loot."

"Good girl." He patted her hand and matched her smile.

"It's not though, is it? Good I mean."

The smile didn't leave his face, but she knew it was all on the outside.

"You got a better plan?" He asked it so gently, so calmly that she almost forgot what happened to people who questioned Bryan's ideas.

"Would you listen if I had?"

"'Course not. Girls aren't no good at planning. Don't worry yourself though, Cupcake. Just do as Bryan says and we'll be going up in the world."

They rode the up escalator. As they passed the beauty counter where Cindy had once longed to work, she couldn't help glancing in.

"No point, Cupcake. They ain't got nothing worth stealing."

Cindy wanted to steal; steal herself away from Bryan. He always found her. Re-educated her where the bruises wouldn't spoil her usefulness as a decoy.

They followed Baz and Fingers into the jeweller's. Cindy was so busy with her chest out and fluttering eyelashes part of the deal she wasn't sure if she'd really seen the flash of red, a glimpse of blue denim through the plate glass. She simpered and fainted.

The plan went perfectly. Fingers left while Cindy was still limp in the manager's strong arms with her chest heaving and her heart pounding. Baz did another circuit of the shop, keeping his head turned away from the CCTV cameras, then slunk away. Bryan offered his arm to Cindy and assurances they'd be back to purchase the ring once she'd got some air and felt up to making a choice.

Bryan held her more firmly than he'd have needed to if she really had been overcome, and 'helped' her reach the exit. Cindy, still playing her part, clung to him and looked around the mass of people as though unsure where she was.

"Don't overdo it," Bryan hissed.

His warning came too late. Someone asked if she was all right, if they could help.

"Just felt a bit dizzy," Cindy said. The sharp pinch from Bryan encouraged her to stand straighter. "I'll be fine in a few minutes."

Cindy had been right; she had seen the man in blue jeans. He didn't appear to have noticed her though and was walking ahead of them towards the exit.

Outside the shopping centre Bryan released his grip on his sister but she didn't delude herself that meant she was free to leave his side. She walked with him into the dark alleyway where they'd arranged to meet Fingers and Baz. Those two were already waiting and looking through the loot. The dazzling gems didn't impress Cindy. The backslapping and shouts of triumph from the men didn't impress her. The quiet words from the man in blue jeans did.

"Armed police. You're under arrest."

Gold bangles, pearl earrings and diamond rings bounced like hailstones on the damp pavement. Their glitter dimmed in the presence of the fluorescent police jackets.

"Bryan Morgan, you're going down," the jeans wearing, plain-clothed police officer said after cuffing Bryan, Baz and Fingers and reading them their rights.

"You're not the only one with a plan, Bryan," Cindy explained. "Mine is witness protection."

11 Spider's Web

"Mum, I want my Spider-Man pyjamas, please."

"OK love, I'll bring them tomorrow."

Bleach had accidentally been spilt. The threadbare material was weak and the strong chemical had ruined them. This was not something Sandy wanted to tell Jamie. He was weak too, connected to a dialysis machine until a new kidney became available. Every day without the operation was a disappointment; it was another day he couldn't play football or walk his dog. She just couldn't disappoint him further.

The following day, Sandy went to the shop where she'd originally bought the pyjamas. They no longer stocked them.

"All the kids are into Caribbean pirates now."

Jamie wasn't, he'd been too ill to go to the cinema. She tried every clothes shop, toy shop and department store in town. She tried the supermarket and the fancy dress hire shop. She was fed up with being offered pirate clothes, eye patches and cutlasses. Sandy bought Jamie a Spider-Man book; she knew he would thank her. He was always polite. He wouldn't complain, he never did.

"It's not fair," she cried.

"What isn't, dear?" an elderly lady asked her.

"Oh sorry, I didn't know I said that aloud. It's nothing."

"Not nothing, you're upset. Come on, a trouble shared and all that."

"My little boy is ill and wants Spider-Man pyjamas. Everywhere sold them a few months ago. Now it seems they've all been thrown away in favour of the latest trend."

"What a waste."

"It's fashion I suppose," Sandy said.

"But they needn't throw them away. They could go to Oxfam or…"

"Of course, why didn't I think of that? Thanks."

Sandy was gone, no doubt leaving a slightly confused woman looking after her.

Sandy went into Oxfam and explained. They didn't have what she wanted, but took her phone number.

"We get donations nearly every day, you might get lucky."

In Save the Children, they had a Spider-Man T-shirt, almost new and only 50p. Jamie would be pleased. She would have given up then, she'd spent time in shops that she would have rather spent with her son. She would have given up, but she passed a Scope shop on the way back to her car.

As she went in a lady with swollen red eyes was handing over a box of clothes.

"Some of this stuff has hardly been worn, it seems wrong to give it away, but my son," she paused to blow her nose. "Sorry, silly of me, I should be getting over this. Well he won't need these things."

Sandy saw the familiar black web on the red material.

"Are they Spider-Man pyjamas?"

"Yes."

"I'll take them."

"Well, they're not priced up or anything. I can't sell them yet," the assistant informed her.

Sandy turned to the lady who had brought them in.

"Look, technically they're still yours, as you haven't left them here yet. Please sell them to me. My son is very, very sick. Please."

"Well, you have a point, they are mine. Tell you what, you put something in the collection box and I'll give them to you." She turned to the shop worker, "That's fair isn't it, Dorothy?"

Sandy opened her purse and took out a £10 note.

"Do you want change?"

"No, this is a bargain."

Sandy rushed home and put the new clothes into the washing machine. Leaving her husband a note, she took the book to her son.

"Your pyjamas are in the wash, Daddy will bring them this evening, and a T- shirt."

"Brilliant, thanks, Mum."

Jamie's dad did bring the clothes, but Jamie didn't get to wear them that night. Instead, he wore a plain theatre gown. The orderly who collected him heard him wishing he could wear his Spider-Man outfit for good luck in the operation.

"You can't see the back of your gown, can you lad?"

"No, why?"

"That's a special Spider-Man gown. Even Spider-Man might get hurt and need to come to hospital."

"Really?"

"Oh yes, it's got the web and everything."

"You never said, Mum."

"She probably can't see it. It's in special ink, only really special people can see it."

"Like you?"

"No lad, I can't, but it's in your notes see. As you're his best fan he wanted you to have special spider luck to make the operation work really well."

"Wow!"

The orderly left him with his parents for a few minutes outside the theatre. He came out again, smiling reassuringly at Jamie's parents.

"They're all set for you now lad. Mum and Dad will stay with you 'til you're asleep, next thing you'll know the op. will be over and they'll be sat by the side of your bed. You'll have tubes and stuff in you, don't worry about that, they're to help you get well. Your parents will look worried, don't worry about that either, that's their job."

He wheeled the bed into the operating theatre.

"Hello, Jamie," said the surgeon, "Hey I didn't realise you were a friend of Spider-Man's."

"How did you know?"

"You're wearing his gown."

"You can see the web?"

"Yes. You must be very special to get to wear that."

"Mum, it's going to be all right, if he can see the web he can fix me. He's got special powers."

"Of course he has."

Sandy and her husband held Jamie's hands as the anaesthetic was administered, kissed him as he became drowsy, then were ushered outside to wait.

The transplant operation was completely successful and Jamie was home in advance of the hospital's predictions. It was then Sandy remembered the lady with the red eyes. The lady who's son would never again be tucked into bed by his mum, wearing Spiderman pyjamas. She went back to the shop.

"Dorothy?"

"Sorry, do I know you?"

"No, but I bought some Spiderman pyjamas here a while ago. I think the person who brought them in was a friend of yours. I'd really like to speak to her."

"I remember you now. Well you're in luck, she's coming to collect me after I finish here. I'll give her a ring and ask her to come a bit earlier. Shall we say twenty to five?"

Sandy told Dorothy's friend how much better Jamie was and how the pyjamas had boosted his morale, possibly helping his recovery. "I feel so bad. I just snatched them and ran. That was heartless, you must have been so upset and I never gave you a thought. I just wanted to say sorry."

"I'm glad your boy is on the mend, but I don't quite understand what you're apologising for."

"I suppose I feel guilty that I have a son recovering, when you don't. Getting what I want for my son seems to mean another mother suffers."

"My son is not recovering because he hasn't been ill."

"But you were crying and said that he wouldn't need the clothes."

"I suffer with hay fever. And he didn't need them, because he has abandoned Spiderman in favour of pirates. No one died."

"Oh! I'm so glad."

"Well, me too. What was the operation that saved your boy?"

"Kidney transplant."

The two mothers looked at each other. They both knew that although they had sons at home, a mother somewhere did not. They could only hope that Jamie's new chance at life would be of comfort, and that they would never know her sorrow.

12 Give And Take

Penny Cooper had been my friend since we started infant school. She'd grabbed my hand the moment we were introduced.

"Hello, Anna Pound, you're going to be my friend," she said.

That's what she was like, if she saw something she wanted, she just walked up and grabbed it. If she wanted a particular story book, that's the one she picked up. If she liked what was in my lunch box, better than whatever her mother had given her, then we swapped. We played whichever games Penny wanted to play. It just never occurred to her that anyone wouldn't want to go along with her wishes. She was usually right; I was happy to follow along in her wake.

We did almost everything together. Our parents and the teachers soon got used to treating us as a pair. "In for a Penny, in for a Pound," they'd joke whenever one of us wanted to do anything or go anywhere. Our similar tastes weren't always a good thing, not for me anyway. Boys I liked all too often became Penny's boyfriends. It wasn't just with lads; Penny would take a liking to whatever I'd got my eye on. If I pointed out a hairstyle I fancied, or a stunning dress, next thing I knew, she'd have a new look.

Once we both bought lottery tickets.

"Let's have a look at your numbers then," Penny said as she grabbed my ticket. "Oh, twenty-seven, I wish I'd got that one, as that's my birthday."

Of course, we swapped cards. I won £10 with mine, but I didn't win one over on Penny. She said the drinks were on me and promptly ordered a £15 bottle of wine.

I've made her sound greedy and grasping, haven't I? She isn't now, and to be honest, she wasn't even when we were kids. Although she might have wanted to play with my latest toy, she was happy to share all hers with me, even brand-new ones. If she ate my apple, she replaced it with her orange, sometimes adding a packet of crisps too.

Once I arrived at her house ready for a night out and saw I'd spilt something on my top.

"Grab whatever you like from the wardrobe," she'd offered. When I pulled out a shiny top with an incredibly high price tag still attached, she didn't flinch. "Try it on, Anna. It'll look great on you."

She was right, it did. We weren't the only ones who thought so; Brian agreed. She never tried to take him away from me and when we married, my 'something borrowed' came from her.

Penny always did have a way of stealing the limelight though. The time I was picked as Mary in the school play, it was Penny as the inn-keeper who got the good lines and her picture in the school newsletter. When I gave birth, after fourteen hours in labour, it was Penny who got her picture in the paper. There had been a flash flood in our village and the roads were impassable to everyone but Penny. She borrowed her kid brother's inflatable dinghy, blew it up with a bicycle pump and rowed me to somewhere reachable by ambulance. Brian had been trapped at his office by the same flood, so Penny held my hand and muttered encouragement for hours until he could reach my side.

When Penny saw my beautiful son, she fell for him instantly. "I'm going to take him away from you," she said.

She did too; but only when it suited me. She was a great babysitter. When Dominic got older, she indulged him with crazy gifts and outrageous treats.

"Remember that mummies and daddies have to be sensible; only Aunty Penny is allowed to buy you a spaceman suit, or take you driving in a racing car," she told him.

When Dominic became ill, Penny shared my pain.

"When I was a kid, I always took things away from you. If I could take away this horrible disease, then I would."

I hugged her; I knew she meant it. She did try too. She went for the blood test to see if she would make a suitable bone marrow donor. So did our friends and families; everyone that knew us and thousands who didn't. Penny helped us contact local TV, radio, and papers to ask for people to register as donors. She tweeted, posted on Facebook and set up a website.

We were on a girlie day out, Penny's treat to cheer me up, when Brian called from the hospital.

"Anna, they've got one!" he yelled. "I've just heard they've found a good match. He's got a chance; our boy has got a chance."

Penny took the phone and wiped my tears as she waited to hear if I was crying with joy or sorrow.

"We need to go to the hospital," was all I could say, but I'm sure my expression told her all she needed to know.

Next thing I knew, she'd stuck me in the car and started driving. Her smile was as big as my own. I didn't know if Penny was the match, that didn't matter. All that mattered was that Dominic now had a second chance and Penny would be with us to share every moment.

13 Going Uphill Slowly

Billy watched the last of the snow melt away. It made him a little sad, reminding him his youth too had melted away and all his boyhood adventures were lost in the past. He laughed at his own thoughts. Billy was seventy-eight; his youth hadn't just melted it had evaporated. He wasn't in bad nick though. Helping round the house kept him fit and healthy. Games and conversation with George kept his mind active. Even his sight was OK now he'd got new glasses. Life was pretty fine. He'd like another adventure though.

He was glad the snow had gone, dangerous stuff it was for an old chap like him; one fall and his already painful hip would be no use at all. If things were bad for Billy, how much worse must they be for young George? At least Billy had enjoyed several winters of sledging down Battle Hill; George would never get the chance. Billy couldn't even pronounce what was wrong with the poor lad's legs.

Together they'd played Scrabble and assembled jigsaws whilst the snow had fallen outside. They'd tried not to mind they were stuck indoors, whilst kids struggled up the steep slippery hill and whooshed down on a variety of sledges, trays and even plastic sacks.

It was the first winter in years that Billy had spent in his childhood home. He'd left, aged seventeen, to join the army. At first he'd come back regularly to visit his parents, but they were gone now. The house was still in the family, his great niece Natasha owned it and lived there with her son George. She'd invited Billy to spend Christmas with her. He'd been tempted; he didn't enjoy life in his sheltered accommodation. It was boring. Having nothing to do meant he concentrated on his minor aches and pains, his poor eyesight and weakening memory. He'd started to feel he was going downhill fast. Billy didn't like to impose though, Natasha was a kind woman, but had enough work raising her son single-handed. Eventually, she'd persuaded Billy to visit for a week in the new year. After six days, she'd asked him to stay permanently.

"I know you're not happy where you are and there's more than enough room for you here."

"It's not so bad there, just a bit lonely maybe. Anyway, I don't want to put you to any trouble."

"You'd not be any trouble, Uncle Billy. Whilst you've been here, you've done more than your share of housework and you're great with George. Knowing you'd be here when he came home from school would be wonderful; it's often a real struggle to get away from work on time."

"I'd love to stay here for a while. It would do me good to feel useful. I could pay my way too, but what'll happen if I get sick or summat and need more care? Thanks, Natasha, but I must say no. I can't become a burden to you."

"Uncle Billy, it might not ever come to that, but if it does… Look, how about if I promise that the minute I'm finding it hard work to have you around, I arrange for you to go into a local home? You said the problem with the place you're in now is loneliness. If you were close by, I could visit you much more often."

Billy hadn't needed much persuading. He did return to his old accommodation, but only for long enough to pack and sort out the paperwork.

He'd been living with Natasha and George for three weeks when the snow started. Billy and George had watched with sadness as children, and some parents, sledged down the hill.

They could hear the squeals of excitement and laughter as one after another, people raced down the hill, either stopping neatly or crashing into bushes and loose snow.

"Trekking through the snow, climbing Battle Hill and whizzing to the bottom would be pretty cool," George said.

"We can't do that, lad."

"I know, Uncle Billy. We might get hurt if we went downhill fast."

Billy had laughed. "Do you know, I thought I was doing just that before I moved here?"

"What do you mean?"

"That I was falling apart, going downhill fast."

George had laughed too, once he'd understood. "But you're not now, are you?"

"No, I'm on the up, even if I am a bit slow."

"Going up slow is better than going downhill fast, then?"

"I suppose so, lad," Billy said. That's when he'd got the idea. He'd use his old military skills to plan and carry out an adventure with George. He spoke to Natasha then waited for the snow to melt.

On the first dry, sunny weekend of the year, Billy and George got up early for a proper cooked breakfast.

"Eat up, you'll need your strength, boys," Natasha had said as she placed steaming plates of bacon, eggs, tomatoes, mushrooms and toast in front of George and Billy.

"What are we doing? Come on, you'll have to tell me soon," George said.

"We're going on an expedition," Billy said.

"Wow! Really? Where to? Are we going now? How will we get there?"

Natasha laughed. "Calm down, George! I'll load your

supplies and you pay attention to your expedition brief."

Together, George and Billy set off across the park. They each had their sticks to help them and a backpack of supplies. On the level mown grass, they made good progress. At the edge of the park, they rested on a bench and took on fluids, from their water bottles. When they were ready, they negotiated the first obstacle; a stile. They climbed carefully and helped each other. It wasn't long before they'd started on the ascent.

The climb was hard; the two explorers had to take care not to trip on the rough ground or slip on the steep incline. They needed frequent breaks. Each time they reached a bench, they rested, drank water to stay hydrated, ate mints for energy and congratulated each other on how far they'd got.

"I never thought I'd go climbing again, George."

"I didn't think I'd do it, ever, Uncle Billy."

Occasionally, Billy tested communications, by calling Natasha on his mobile and reporting on their progress. It took a long time to reach the summit and they were very tired. They sat side by side on the grass, not speaking, just smiling.

Natasha arrived to offer a lift back to base camp just as they'd finished slapping each other on the back and admiring the view and their achievement. She took a photograph of them both, with nothing but the pale blue sky behind them.

"I'll print us a copy each."

After that, Billy continued to age, George still had bad legs and Natasha worked hard to care for them. Usually life was fine, but whenever one of them thought things were going downhill fast, they'd take out the picture and remember they could choose to go uphill slowly.

14 Fish Food

Although her lunch break was officially over, Melanie gazed out the kitchen window instead of hurrying downstairs to her brother's pet shop. Work forgotten, she watched a child sail a boat on the small pond. How lovely to play outside on the weekends instead of being forced to work. How wonderful not to be surrounded by fish all day.

"Melanie!" Pete called up. "As you're still up there, could you make me a cup of tea?"

It wasn't fair, the sun was shining now. If she'd taken the second break she could have eaten her sandwiches in the park instead of the flat over the shop. In that case, he'd have been the one making the tea and carrying one down for her, not the other way around. She sighed and filled the kettle.

"Thanks," Pete said as he took the mug from her.

He was a good brother really, even if he did make her work. He didn't complain too much when she was late. Mind you, it wasn't her fault anyway; there were just so many interesting things to look at on the way. Of course she wouldn't be late if she had the car she was saving for as her attention would be on the road. Then again, she wouldn't need the job once she'd bought the car. She'd hoped her dad or brother would lend her the money.

"No, Melanie," Pete said. "It would do you good to work for something, for a change."

"I work at college," she'd tried to convince him.

"Sorry, love. Pete's right," was all their dad would say.

"Melanie, are you listening to me?" Pete asked now.

"Yes, sort of. What did you say?"

"That I'm going to lunch now," Pete said. "Perhaps you could start pricing up the new stock whilst I'm gone?"

"OK."

"Please do as much as you can and not just a couple of things before you get distracted."

"OK," Melanie said, looking at the neatly arranged stock. There was an awful lot of new stuff; most of it fish care products. She'd been right to take the earlier break and get out of unpacking it all.

"Oh and don't forget that Mrs Rotherstone will be in later. Give me a call if she comes in before I'm back down," Pete said and stood up.

No, not Mrs Rotherstone!

Melanie turned the chair Pete had vacated, so she wouldn't see the fish tanks when she sat in it.

"I'll be back at half past two," Pete added as he headed for the stairs.

"Half past?"

"Yes, for some reason, I seem to be starting my break later than usual."

Melanie scowled at his back. Why hadn't he taken his lunch break earlier and why hadn't he told her Mrs Rotherstone was coming in? And he'd cleared off and left her with all the work to do. She stuck price tags on two packs of smelly fish food before she heard a rattling noise and went to watch a hamster running round and round on his wheel. She knew how he felt; trapped.

Why was Mrs Rotherstone coming? The woman got on Melanie's nerves; she constantly criticised. It had started when Melanie was eleven and Mrs Rotherstone had been her maths teacher. 'Melanie is very intelligent and extremely lazy. If she can learn to concentrate and work hard, she will do well', was written in her report the first year. 'Melanie's good grades are the result of natural ability and no reflection on the minimal effort she puts into her school work' had been her opinion the second year. Melanie had tried, but it was a struggle. She was expected to concentrate all day in her lessons and then when she got home, she was expected to do even more work, yet there were so many other interesting things she wanted to do.

When her exam results had arrived, Mrs Rotherstone had visited Melanie's dad.

"Thanks to the extra effort she has put in recently, Melanie has done reasonably well but she's capable of much better; she needs to learn to concentrate."

Her dad had agreed. Because of Mrs Rotherstone, Melanie was now slaving away at college, instead of taking the gap year she'd hoped for. Because of her, she was forced to work for her brother. Pete made her serve on the till and carry things and clean and feed the pets; the list of jobs was endless and very dull. He hardly ever let her take a break either. It was awful.

If it hadn't been for Mrs Rotherstone, Melanie could have earned her money far more easily. She'd seen an advert for house-sitting. That would have suited her very well; all she'd have had to do was water plants and stack up the mail for the owners. The rest of the time she could do some of the interesting things she never had time for, or perhaps just watch their TVs, read their books and eat their food. It would have been the perfect job.

Melanie's big mistake was to tell Mrs Rotherstone. They'd bumped into each other in town.

"How are you finding college?" her former teacher had asked.

Worried she might question her about homework, or even suggest private tutoring, Melanie had tried to distract her by mentioning her planned new job.

"What a wonderful idea, Melanie! I have a weekend break booked, perhaps I could be your first customer?"

Melanie had arrived almost early at Mrs Rotherstone's house. She'd told Melanie that many of her friends were interested in using Melanie's services over the holidays.

"If you wanted to, you could be fully booked for the whole six weeks."

As her first customer gave Melanie detailed instructions for care of the house, Melanie had daydreamed of her summer break. For six weeks she could be paid to be in other people's houses and she wouldn't have to worry about a thing. She'd soon have enough money for her car.

"…that could happen any day now; please don't worry if it does. Melanie? Are you are listening to me?" Mrs Rotherstone's voice interrupted Melanie's plans.

"Oh, yes. It could happen any day; I understand."

Melanie had no idea what the other woman had been talking about, but as she'd told Melanie not to worry, it couldn't have been important.

"Perhaps your brother would know what to do about the fish?"

Mrs Rotherstone must have been saying that Pete could tell her how to look after the fish if she had any questions.

"Oh, yes of course, don't worry about that."

Things had gone well from the start. After watching one of Mrs Rotherstone's DVDs, Melanie took a look around the house. She noticed pot plants, but decided to water them later. There weren't any pets to worry about, except the fish. She gave it a nice big pinch of food so she wouldn't have to go near it again. Her work finished, Melanie ordered a pizza and settled down with a book she'd had for weeks but no time to read. Over the following two days, Melanie had relaxed completely and enjoyed herself very much.

Four hours before Mrs Rotherstone was due home, Melanie walked round the house to check all was well. It wasn't; she'd forgotten the house plants. Pots of herbs wilted on the windowsill and Melanie had to rush round the house watering every plant she could find. Then she found the fish dead in his tank. Poor Mrs Rotherstone, since her son had left home, the fish was the only company she had. The poor woman would be devastated. In a panic Melanie had rung Pete.

"You have to help me. Please, I'll do anything!"

"What kind of fish is it?"

"A dead one! I don't know, it's just a fish."

Just for a moment, Melanie regretted never having taken any interest in the family business. She raced to the tank and studied the dead creature.

"It's striped black and white and it's got pointy bits. It's flat now, but it was the other way up before and looked thin. I gave it lots of food though, it didn't starve, Pete."

"It's far more likely you over fed it."

"Oh no! Did I kill it?"

"I don't know what's wrong with it without even seeing it. Shall I come round?"

"A post-mortem won't help me; I need a new fish."

"From your description, I think it's an angel fish. I sold her one like that several years…"

"I don't care when it was; can you get another one?"

"Luckily, I have one just like it."

Pete had agreed to help her, if she would agree to help him in his shop.

"I'll do anything!"

Melanie donned rubber gloves, scooped out the dead fish and carried it, at arm's length, to the cloakroom. She quickly flushed it down the toilet.

The new fish was swimming in the tank and Pete was out of sight with just minutes to spare.

Mrs Rotherstone had been pleased with the exhausted Melanie and repeated the offer to pass on Melanie's details to other teachers. Melanie had been forced to decline any further work.

"Sorry, but I'm going to be working in my brother's shop."

That had been months ago. Since then Melanie had worked full-time in the pet shop for the rest of what was the summer holidays for everyone else and during every weekend since.

The pet shop door opened and the arrival of the source of Melanie's unhappy memories walked into the shop.

"Mrs Rotherstone, how nice to see you," she said as cheerfully as she could. "Have you come for some fish food?"

"I'm afraid I won't be needing any of that any more."

"Oh dear. Has something awful happened to your lovely fish?"

"My fish is dead, but there's no need to be upset. He was very old; in fact he'd lived much longer than I'd expected. You might remember me saying?"

"No." Melanie had tried to erase every thought of Mrs Rotherstone's fish from her thoughts.

"When you came to house-sit for me, I told you not to

worry if anything happened to him as he'd already lived far longer than captive fish are expected to."

"Oh."

"I had a feeling at the time that you weren't listening. That's why I called in to see your brother and tell him to reassure you if the fish died. You never did concentrate very well, did you? You didn't use to work very well either, so I'm pleased…"

As Mrs Rotherstone went on about being pleased Melanie now had a job and that she'd heard her grades were much better, Melanie gazed around the shop. She'd so far avoided looking at the angel fish, swimming contentedly in their tank, but now they had her attention. It wasn't the fish that interested her, but the price tag on the front. The very low price tag.

"Mrs Rotherstone, I'm sorry to interrupt, but Pete asked me to call him when you came in."

Melanie went to the doorway. "Pete!" When her brother arrived, Melanie said, "Mrs Rotherstone has just been telling me about her fish."

"Oh?" Pete asked.

"About how it was very old when I went to house-sit and how you knew she wasn't expecting it to last much longer."

"That's right, she did tell me that," Pete agreed. "She also told me how you needed to learn to concentrate and work hard. That's why I thought working here would be good for you. It means you have less distractions in your life and you also finish all your homework as a way of getting out of looking after the fish."

"You've lied to me and you've had me working here for months for nothing and…"

"No he hasn't," Mrs Rotherstone said. "We both tried to

tell you about the fish, but you didn't listen."

"Oh." Melanie thought about all the times her brother, and her teacher come to that, had tried to tell her things and she hadn't listened. "You're right. I don't concentrate. I see now that I should."

"Good," Pete said.

"All right, you've taught me a lesson about concentrating, but what about work? You've both said I should work and I've worked here for months and all for nothing."

"Not for nothing," Pete said. "I said you had to work here, but I didn't say I wouldn't pay you. I reckon three months back pay should be just about enough for the deposit on the car you wanted."

Melanie rushed out of the shop. She'd only gone a few yards when she realised she still had half a day to work and that her brother and Mrs Rotherstone might still have advice to offer. She went back and half listened to them as they instructed her how to calculate the profit margins on fish food and wondered what colour car to buy. It definitely wouldn't be salmon or gold or anything else connected with fish.

15 Uncle's House

I looked at the house and then back to the estate agent's notes in my hands. Could this dingy depressing place really be worth £340, 000? That sum of money would make a huge difference to my business. I was doing OK but a cash injection like that would put me on a whole new level. Help pick me up, as Uncle Alfred would say. I walked on to my uncle's house just three doors down. His was the end of the row, a little larger, a little more valuable.

Uncle Alfred greeted me eagerly. "Oh, Tony my boy, it's so long since I saw you." I had anticipated such a remark and he must have seen a reaction in my face.

He rushed on, "Oh don't worry, boy. I know how it is, you're a busy lad. I'm glad to see you whenever you're able to spare the time."

He ushered me in, hung up my jacket and took my case upstairs. He fussed about, fretting over pillows and extra blankets. I don't know why, the old boy was probably preparing for my visit since I phoned him last week. Downstairs he made us tea; too strong and too sweet. He asked if I was hungry and I offered to get fish and chips for us both. He was suitably grateful. Truth is there was no way I would eat any of the overcooked rubbish he'd dish up. It was bad enough having the depressing atmosphere of old age and poverty entering through my eyes, nose and ears. I wouldn't swallow it down inside my expensively cared for fit, young body.

"Oh, thanks for the money towards the roof my, boy," he mumbled as he put our food onto plates.

I told him it was nothing and that was nearly true. What was a couple of hundred quid to protect my inheritance? When I sent the cheque I'd done it really to keep the old boy quiet and to ease my conscience too, I suppose. If I'd seen those estate agent's details earlier I would have written it with less regret for the nice dinner it could have bought. Having to boycott the club for one night was a small price to pay for ensuring my uncle had a sound roof over his home. My home too I suppose. He'd taken me in after my father was sent to prison. My mother had been able to cope with mixing a vodka martini but not with making a sandwich for my lunch.

Uncle Alfred had told me very little about my parents except that I should not be ashamed. I was his boy now and everything would be all right. It had never occurred to me before to be ashamed of my parents. They'd both been rich, successful, well dressed. They had loads of friends and I had everything I wanted, even if it was the home help or Dad's PA who provided it and sent in a bill. My parents were busy, of course and spent more time with their friends than with me, but when they returned they always had gifts for me. Then my dad got caught out in his latest scam. Of course I was ashamed then; he was a failure and I had to go and live with his hard up, boring brother.

My uncle was always there for me. I couldn't get away from him as he tried to make up for my careless upbringing and the loss of my parents. Eventually I gained a grudging respect for him. I followed his advice to 'pick myself up and carry on'. I worked hard at school and started a respectable, honest, investment business. I wouldn't make my father's mistake, I always stayed technically, if not ethically, within the law.

I showed my uncle the details for his neighbour's house. He was full of regret that another set of the 'old originals' was moving away. Like him, Mr and Mrs Blenkinsopp had moved into the street when it was newly built. They were moving out into sheltered accommodation now.

"That's why the house is being sold. Cost a fortune these places, there'll be nothing left for the kids in a year or two. Doesn't seem right."

"That doesn't matter though, the money I mean. As long as their parents are happy and well looked after I'm sure the family don't begrudge a bit of cash." I said what I hoped he wanted to hear.

"That's as maybe, my boy, still I'll miss them. Good neighbours were the Blenkinsopps."

"Uncle, this has given me an idea. Look, I've been worried about you for a while."

"No need, Tony lad. I'm fine as I am."

"But this house is a lot of work for you. It's starting to need a lot of work, the roof… The windows could do with replacing and the wiring wants looking at. I'll help you, you know I will, but it's still a worry for you. Wouldn't you be happier somewhere modern, with everything taken care of?"

"No! Never. I won't be carted off to some home to sit around and rot."

"Of course not, I meant a decent place. Maybe you could move in next to the Blenkinsopps. You'd like that wouldn't you?"

"No!"

"But I worry about you. What if you had a fall?"

"I'd pick myself up and carry on. I'll not go into a home. This place will be yours when I'm gone but I'll not leave here."

"All right, Uncle, we'll not argue about it. But think about what I've said and if you should change your mind let me know. I'll pay for it, you wouldn't have to sell. The house will stay in the family."

"Tony, my boy, I know you mean well. Let's not talk about it again." He switched on the television, effectively ending the discussion.

After a couple of hours of dumbed down quizzes and a sit-com with an unbelievable situation and no comedy I went to bed.

I wanted Uncle Alfred to live somewhere safe. I didn't like to know he had no one but me to call if he had any kind of problem. I couldn't always come rushing to his aid at a moment's notice. I wanted the money the sale of his house would bring too. The cost of his care would easily be met from the profits of that kind of investment. It would be better for both of us if he left his old house but I didn't know how to make him see that.

As I came out of the bathroom the following morning I saw my uncle clutching the banister for support. He was bent over a bit more than usual and in obvious pain.

He realised I'd seen this. "Don't look like that, my boy. My arthritis is always a bit worse in the mornings that's all, nothing to worry about. I'm fine once I get going."

"Uncle, you're not fine. You can hardly walk. I know you're a proud man but you need a bit of help."

"No! No I don't. I'm not proud, I'm independent. I'll not have any meddling in my life. I will never go into a home. This house will be yours when I die but until that day I will stay here. Whatever life throws at me I will pick myself up and carry on." His wry smile assured me that he knew and meant exactly what he said.

I walked over to him and put my hand on his shoulder.

"All right, Uncle. You will live here just as you are until

the day you die. I shall see to it."

"Thanks, Tony my boy."

We looked at each other, both remembering the many years we'd spent there together. We hugged briefly then, embarrassed by this unusually intimate act, stepped awkwardly away from each other.

Uncle lost his footing; he teetered slowly, silently like an action replay for a few moments before crashing backwards down the stairs. He struck his head on the tiled hallway and somersaulted over. No one lying with his neck bent back like that could possibly be still living.

"Pick yourself up from that then, Uncle."

I called an ambulance immediately and waited with him until it came to take his body away. I waited almost a week before taking his will and the deeds to my solicitor. It took over a month before I was once again holding estate agent's literature, but the asking price for Uncle's house made all the waiting worthwhile.

16 Family Recipe

I fetch the ceramic mixing bowl from the garage. It's too heavy for everyday use, so for most of the year it's put away. It only comes out when I mix together the Christmas pudding ingredients. My grandma used this bowl to make her Christmas puddings before she passed it on to my mother. The bowl is mine now. I've taught my own daughters, Sally and Carol, to make puddings according to the family recipe.

As I run water to clean it, before making this year's batch, I'm reminded I can't keep doing this for much longer. My arthritic hands find difficulty in holding the bowl steady. I have to squint to read the measurements on the scales and stirring the mix has become hard work. One of my daughters will have to take on the task. As they're twins, it's not obvious which. I guess Sally will volunteer; she's always ready to accept responsibility. She'd take good care of this treasured piece of china. Carol would worry more about what it represents, she might not always manage to make the puddings months in advance, or stick precisely to the recipe, but she'd always produce something and she'd do it with passion. I rather hope they'll find a way to share the bowl, possibly taking turns to make the puddings.

I dry the cream coloured surface and place the bowl on the table. I'm not sure how many puddings I've mixed in this bowl; at least one a year, but often more. When my brother Allen emigrated, he took a pudding with him for the first Christmas he spent with his new family. Each subsequent year, he received another pudding. I make them early, so holidaying visitors can take them.

The mixing bowl and recipe will be handed on for generations, unless one of us breaks it before then. I can't imagine that happening. It's been dropped before, but there are no chips or cracks. I used to think both it and my family were indestructible but, of course, that's not true.

As I begin to assemble the ingredients, the familiar routine seems more than a bringing together of foodstuffs. It's almost as if I'm drawing my family to me. I suppose that's true in a way; even when separated the traditional dessert keeps us in each other's thoughts. To prove the truth of this, the phone rings. As I make my way to the hall, I wonder if it's Sally to reassure me they're on their way, or Carol to inform me about whatever crisis has delayed them.

"There's a slight change of plan," Sally says. "Don't worry, we're coming, but Carol's got a minor problem over the kids' football practice. I'm leaving now and Carol will follow as soon as she can."

I chuckle; amused at my girls acting so completely in character. They'll never change.

As I return to the kitchen, I think about things which have changed. I now buy the nuts shelled ready for use. I weigh each item on electronic scales, not the metal balance my grandma used. The cooked puddings are sealed in convenient plastic containers, rather than wrapped in layers of muslin and waxed papers for storage. Last year, I tried microwaving part of the mixture. It was so much easier than hours of steaming, quicker with no chance of boiling dry either. The result was excellent, so that's how they'll be done in future.

The ingredients haven't changed much. I still a use a little suet, although now it comes ready shredded in boxes and is clean and odourless. Suet isn't popular in these modern low-fat times, but it's vital to create the perfect texture. I bought some fresh this week and felt rather old fashioned as a result. The young assistant in the Co-op had never heard of suet. When I explained what it was and why I wanted it, she patiently informed me there was no need to make them, as they could be bought ready-made in December. She stressed December as though advance preparation was something to be ashamed of and as though she didn't realise puddings, mince pies and snowily iced cakes had been on sale since September. Like family traditions and the older generation suet is an ingredient which can be taken for granted; forgotten almost until Christmas, when it's at last appreciated. I use real butter too; margarine just doesn't give that full, rich flavour.

Next is plain flour, which seems so basic and dull. It's the routine of daily life. Little things such as good manners and keeping in touch seem dreary compared to big celebrations and exciting events but it's how we treat each other every day which holds us together as a family. The heavy bag is tucked away in the corner cupboard. There's a little effort involved in bringing it to the table. The pudding would just be a pile of sticky fruit without good old boring flour to hold it together. I add some raising agent; a little can make a big difference in the same way an unexpected visit or someone taking a little extra trouble over your happiness can lift your day from ordinary to joyful. Belatedly I check the sell-by date as I can't remember when I bought this pack. It's fine, some things really last a long time.

I can't resist taking a pinch of the muscovado sugar; I enjoy the sticky texture and delicious flavour. Sugar is sweet, like love. Sugar on its own is sickly and cloying. Our love isn't like that; it's always there, but not heaped on without relief.

A squeeze of fresh lemon and a grating of peel add zest to

cut through the rich flavour. I run hot water from the tap over the lemon, to remove the protective wax coating and to encourage the juice to flow freely.

Some years there's no big pudding made. The family is separated. We share the same love as if we were all together; we share the same batch of mix, divided as we are into smaller pieces. That reminds me of the spices. When mixed together the ginger and cloves sound and smell deliciously exotic. The lives of my family are interesting to hear about. There's sadness too, when anyone is missing at a wedding or for a birthday. If you dab a little of the spice mix on your tongue you'll find its taste is sharp and bitter; it lingers like the sadness of a parting, but adds piquancy to the recipe, recalling sweet reunions.

Then there are the silver coins, added just for fun. Carefully, I polish each one until it shines, before remembering they can't go in the microwave. Ah well, the pudding will taste just the same without them. Fun is important though and should never be missed out; we'll tell jokes as we mix.

Nuts provide some much needed character. They're the kindly old uncles with their tall tales and deep pockets. Every family has a nut or two. Cherries go in as well. They are so pretty and included for their good looks and distinctive texture. They are little girls dressed up for a party, a bride before she walks down the aisle, your lover as he smiles at you in the morning.

I like to include plenty of fruit, plump juicy raisins and sultanas, made deliciously sweet by sun and rich ground. My family has worked hard, we've prospered and grown. I'll sprinkle in a few currants. They're less popular, withered and toughened because they've grown away from the good pastures. I think of the years I've been separated from

Daniel, my younger brother. I've not seen him for so long. He doesn't reply to my letters. I miss him. I'm glad my daughters are so close, both geographically and emotionally.

Again, thinking about the girls has brought one of them to me.

"Hello, love, how are you?" I ask Sally as I hug her.

"In fine cake making form, you?"

I assure her I'm well.

"So have you decided who is to take the mixing bowl and continue the tradition?" I ask.

"Well, sort of. Let's talk about that once Carol gets here."

Oh dear, it doesn't sound as though they've taken me seriously. I was the same when the bowl was passed to me, unwilling to accept the responsibility, unwilling to accept my own mother must relinquish it.

"Sally," I say, "look at these hands; they're too old and weak to cope with that bowl."

"Don't worry, Mum. We've got a plan."

I don't like the sound of that.

The girls are helping me, not just because increasing age means I find it hard work, but for a different and far better reason. This year's pudding is to be the biggest ever. We've had to buy a new plastic bowl to microwave it in. I hope they don't imagine the pudding could be mixed in a plastic bowl? That just wouldn't be the same. No, I'm sure they value the history of this bowl as much as I do. What then, can they have in mind? I try not to worry about that and concentrate instead on the pudding.

Once it is cooked, I'll sprinkle on a little brandy to help preserve it. Then it will be left to mature. A good pudding develops its real flavour over time. Christmas puddings, like good relationships, cannot be made instantly.

I've decided to type the recipe on the computer and print out a copy for any family member who is interested. We have my grandma's original recipe, but the faded handwriting is now difficult to read and there have been a few small amendments made since her day. I'll include the recipes for rum sauce, custard and brandy butter too. Although we all love the pudding, there are differences in our preferred toppings. Clotted or whipped cream is popular too and some of the youngsters favour ice cream. We all agree on the sprig of holly and the ritual of switching off the lights to watch the dancing blue flames of warmed spirit.

I hear a car outside; Carol has arrived. Her sister rushes to meet her, probably deciding how they'll break the news of their plan.

"I'm glad you're both here to help," I say, before either of them can say anything to spoil this afternoon.

"Didn't think we'd let you take all the credit did you?" Carol laughed.

The girls and I are soon weighing ingredients, chopping fruit and beating eggs. We reminisce over previous times we've done this together. Progress is slow as we often stop to wipe tears of laughter from our eyes. At last, almost everything is done. There's just the final magic ingredient to add before we can prepare to cook. In turn, we each take the wooden spoon and stir in wishes for ourselves and everyone else who will share the pudding. Once this is done, the mixture is put into the new bowl and cooked. We clear up and sit down to enjoy a well-deserved cup of tea. We talk about the Christmas meal.

Sally and Carol, together with their husbands and children, will be here to eat it. Children, I call them all still; Sally's daughter is the youngest member of the family and she's almost seventeen. Our son will not be away on a ship this year, so he'll be joining us, with his delightful young lady. Allen and his family are coming over from Australia; they'll be staying with Carol. Our spare room will be occupied by Daniel. At last, he's made contact. He'll be here for Christmas.

Once we've drunk our tea I press them for an answer on the issue of the bowl and family traditions.

"We've been thinking about it, Mum," Sally says. "It doesn't seem right for one to have it and not the other."

I agree with her.

"So we have a plan," Carol says.

"The two of you will do it together?" I ask hopefully.

"No," Sally says.

"No?"

"No, Mum. The three of us will. The bowl will stay here and we'll both come every year and help you."

I hug my girls. What a wonderful solution. I tell them about my plan of typing up the recipe. They are enthusiastic and quickly expand the idea.

"Let's make booklets. We could ask everyone to contribute. They could write about Christmases they remember, there are plenty of good stories," Sally suggests.

"And we could have drawings and photos. I could get them printed up quite easily."

"What a lovely idea. After Christmas lunch, as well as a piece of pudding, we'll give everyone a copy of 'The Family Recipe'.

17 Old Family Recipe

I swipe my ID card to activate the shopping trolley.

"Welcome to Buy 'n' Eat!" it squeals. "The best, the fastest, the cheapest, the cleanest supplier of all your needs. We have lots of special offers for you today, but remember these great prices can only be guaranteed until Tuesday, 19th June 2071."

The trolley lists items which are hardly any more expensive than they were last week. Once that's over we get to the shopping part. As messages screech out, I key my responses. I press the green 'confirm' button to verify the number of people in my household and again to state none of them have a food intolerance.

"It is six days since you purchased food from Buy 'n' Eat," the trolley informs me. I'm glad I haven't shopped elsewhere this week and am therefore spared the sales pitch about how much better this store is. They can't all be better, cleaner, faster and cheaper, but nobody's bothered telling the marketing people. Maybe they think we don't know everything is made by the same manufacturers?

"How many days food supply do you require?" the trolley asks.

I type '10' and press 'confirm' hoping that'll be enough. Trying to explain to a shopping trolley I've had a change of plan is no fun.

"Will you be providing meals for guests during this period?"

I glance around before pressing 'yes' and then 'confirm'

again. I've never lied like that before. Not because I'm spectacularly honest; I've just never felt the need and it's never occurred to me I'd get away with it. I only discovered this ruse by accident. I'd watched amazed as my neighbour, Sonia, piled cakes, biscuits and desserts into her trolley, without a word of reproach from the console. Her body mass index is far above the recommended level. Her husband and son are also height/weight disproportionate. I'd wondered how she purchased enough food for them to maintain that situation. I briefly imagined Sonia hacking into, and changing, their medical records. Daft idea; as if there's a way of accessing medical information about ourselves! If we could, there'd be the danger of returning to the crazy years when people could buy dangerous drugs such as aspirin and self-medicate, or worse, choose not to have treatment.

I confess; I deliberately followed Sonia. I deduced she must be doing something to the trolley when she activated it. I watched, hoping I wouldn't discover she was using a fake ID card. I wanted to know her secret; didn't want to have to report her for fraud. She keyed in the usual responses, each of them truthful, until she was asked about guests. She typed '4'. When asked how many days, she typed '7'. I kept watch on her home; perhaps her guests were licensed organo-greens and would bring their own food. No guests ever arrived. She did the same the following week, again guests failed to appear.

I claim nine guests will each be staying for two days. Surely that'll allow me to purchase sufficient fat and sugar? How stupid not to have made the calculation before I began shopping. I'd done no more than determine how much of each item I'd require and checked my credit level was adequate. The recipe book made it seem so easy. Well, it was written in 2016. I suppose things were different back then.

At last, I'm ready for battle. I give the trolley an experimental shove. It's not too bad; a sharp kick to the front wheels frees the mechanism. Provided I don't try a sharp right-handed turn, I'll be OK.

Plain flour is the first item. I've never bought that before and it takes me a while to find it. I have to press the yellow direction request button and suffer the consequences. After a tour of Buy 'n' Eat during which every item that's either new, improved or on special offer is brought to my attention, I'm directed to the vintage ingredients aisle. It's eerily quiet. I can see down to the end of the row. It's nice to get a glimpse of the goods before having to force my way in and grab something from a shelf, but I'm not sure I like the feeling of isolation. The aisle displays items I don't recognise. I'd be interested in seeing what they're for, but don't have time today. Perhaps I'll return and discover the purpose of malt extract, dried yeast granules, extra virgin olive oil and balsamic vinegar. I find the flour; pass the bag over the scanner and into the trolley.

"Warning. This item contains wheat."

I press the red 'accept' button to acknowledge this potential hazard and the green 'confirm,' to agree I'll not allow the flour to be consumed by any person who's intolerant of wheat products.

"Please be aware this item is a basic food constituent and not a complete food item. It must be processed before consumption."

I tap the keypad to 'accept' this information. I'm going to be doing what my grandma would call 'proper cooking'. She often tells me people don't really cook any more, not like they did years ago. I wonder what she'll say when I show her the method in my copy of the old recipe book. It implies not everyone had a microwave! How could they possibly have cooked anything without a microwave?

What's next? A dozen eggs; oh dear. After only three minutes of pushing and a single kicked shin, I grab the six cartons. I press red acknowledging the helpful information the product contains eggs, and green again, to confirm I won't give them to anyone with an intolerance. Another stab at the green key as I agree they'll require processing as they are not a complete food item.

"This item must not be consumed by pregnant persons."

My grandma claims an egg is a complete food item and people ate them for breakfast, sometimes several at a time. She has some funny ideas about food. That's probably why she's been banned from every supermarket in town.

"I repeat; this item must not be consumed by pregnant persons."

Oh dear, the trolley's annoyed now. I'd better stop thinking about Grandma and concentrate. I hit red, then green. I'm more likely to get RSI than suffer an allergic reaction. There isn't a button for, 'shut up and let me get on with my shopping'. I'm beginning to see why my grandma thinks there should be.

I head towards the sugar, taking a deep breath. I know sugar is unhealthy and bad for my teeth, but the trolley still insists on telling me. I wonder if I could alter my personal information to say I'm deaf? Silent nagging would be easier to accept.

Spices next, and surprisingly none of my selection provoke an extra response from the trolley, other than details of a special offer. Pressing the white button allows me to reject the marvellous saving on items I don't want.

I check the book for the next ingredient for the Christmas pudding. I require large quantities of fruit. The trolley should be pleased; fruit is good. As I seize packs of raisins, cherries, sultanas and currants, I wonder about the woman who wrote the recipe book. She was my mum's grandmother and wrote it the year before my mum was born. It was her wish the family recipe be handed down through the generations. The book has been passed on and I know my cousins in England have continued to make the puddings. I'd never actually seen one or eaten it until we spent our holiday with them last year. It tasted wonderful and I decided it was time the Australian branch of the family revived the tradition. I'd been amazed when Cousin James informed me the original mixing bowl was still intact. He's given it to me, in exchange for the promise of a succession of puddings.

I won't let him down; even though half a kilo each of butter and suet are the next items on the list. Careful alignment of my trolley gives me just enough space to snatch four packs of butter. I grit my teeth as I scan them into the trolley and type in responses to the warnings as quickly as possible. 'Confirm,' it's not just fat, but saturated fat. 'Accept', it contains lactose, 'Confirm' I won't give it to anyone who's intolerant. 'Confirm' I do know of Sunseed block and realise it's a healthier alternative. Now comes the really tricky part. I'm not buying Sunseed block as an alternative to butter, I'm buying it as well. I have too. I looked suet up on Google. It's a saturated fat that was obtained from animals. It can't be bought now obviously. Well, possibly on the black market, but not even for the sake of a Christmas pudding will I buy anything from a butcher. Ugh, those people are disgusting. My grandma reckons the Sunseed block will work just as well.

There's just the final ingredient now, or rather ingredients. My grandma doesn't think raising agent is made now. She advised me to look out for bicarbonate of soda and cream of tartar. With names like that, I'm not surprised they've gone out of fashion. I'm also not surprised I have to ask for directions again. I'm treated to another tour and further instruction on the marvels of Buy 'n' Eat, then directed back to the peace of the vintage ingredients section. I locate the raising agent. My grandma was wrong, raising agent is still made. At least, it's still for sale, the tubs look as though they've been here a while. I put one in the trolley.

"Please enter your chemical users' licence number."

I thought they'd got the chemical licence problem fixed. I heard the same message last time I was here. I'd tried to buy some kitchen cleaning fluid and snatched up one that contained bleach. There'd been another super-germ report on the news, so the aisle was packed with desperate shoppers. I just didn't have the strength to fight for a different product, so I'd carried the pack with me whilst I continued shopping. There'd been some mistake when the product details where input, I was informed at the till. The system had thought I'd tried to buy neat bleach. I read the raising agent pack; the only ingredients listed are the cream of tartar and bicarbonate of soda that my grandma mentioned. I try scanning another tub.

"Please enter your chemical users' licence number."

I press the orange query button on the trolley's keypad. I've never known that to be helpful, but there's a first time for everything.

"This product produces an expansive reaction in use. A valid chemical users' licence is required for purchase."

An expansive reaction is the point of the raising agent, so I have to concede there is no error. I hit the white 'cancel' button. I'll need to ask Cousin James to buy it for me; he's got a licence because of his cleaning job.

I'm almost done now. All I have to do is push the trolley

to the exit and have the transportation crate sealed. Thankfully, I'm not pulled over for a random accuracy test. Last time that happened, I had to take everything out of the trolley to be scanned. What a waste of time that was.

"I'm sorry you didn't have time to complete your shopping," the lad on the sealing station says. "Would you like Buy 'n' Eat to make selections for you, based upon your average requirements from the last three months?"

"No thanks, I've finished."

"But how can you have? There isn't any real food here, just a selection of ingredients."

"That's right, I'm going to cook something," I tell him as he inspects the sell by date on the flour; they've got to be careful with slow moving items.

"Really, what?"

I'd like to explain about the recipe book, but I don't. How do you explain Christmas pudding? It'd be so difficult to do it without referring to Christianity and I'm not daft enough to risk arrest for discussing religion in a public place.

"It's an old family recipe," is the closest I can get.

"Thank you for shopping at Buy 'n' Eat," the trolley says. Those things always have to have the last word.

18 An Unfortunate Series Of Accidents

"I'm in something of a quandary, Jemima dear," my batty old aunt said.

"Are you, Aunty Wendy?" I asked. I'd have liked to say something like, 'Makes a change from hideous mauve nylon', or 'Wish you were and you'd stay there' but I had to be tactful. For one thing she's not actually my aunt, but a great, great aunt by marriage. The old and batty bit was right though. She was also incredibly rich and my godmother.

And she hadn't made her will.

"You see wealth such as ours is a privilege, not shared by everyone."

Aunty probably thought she was explaining with that remark. Liking the 'ours' I nodded encouragingly.

"It shouldn't be abused."

"Quite right," I agreed. I had no intention of abusing her money, I just wanted to spend it. When it seemed she had nothing more to add I offered to make us a drink.

"A nice cup of Early Grey would be lovely, but ring down to the kitchen, you don't need to do it."

"I like to be useful," I said. I'd been hoping she suggested I mix a jug of cocktails, but you can't win them all. I'd been doing quite well at manipulating her lately, but not well enough. I'd dropped hints about inviting Mr Milde to dinner. Making friends with the solicitor responsible for Aunty Wendy's will seemed like an excellent plan, so I tactfully mentioned it would reassure her to know her affairs were in order.

"Plenty of time to sort out all that," she'd said.

I'd agreed there was. I had noticed how much her heart tablets looked like breath mints and realised how easy it would be to switch them. Didn't do it though; I'm neither entirely heartless nor completely stupid.

Aunty Wendy had me rattled not long ago when she suggested giving her 'priceless treasures' to a museum or to Huntington Hall, a local tourist attraction. They're not treasures, they're junk. Very valuable junk that I wanted to get my hands on and sell. I did sometimes. The house was so big that some rooms were permanently locked, to save cleaning and heating them. They weren't empty though; most of the stuff was too big for me to shift. I'd taken a few things and locked up behind me. Where was the harm? I knew it would all be mine anyway soon enough.

Most of the more valuable stuff was in rooms we used though. I couldn't just take that. Aunty's eyesight wasn't that good, but her memory was sharp. What I had to do was buy something as similar as I could from a charity shop, make the switch but leave the replacement item precariously balanced. Sooner or later somebody slammed a door, wielded a duster or just got too close and down it came.

Maybe I overdid those little accidents and Aunty Wendy thought the antiques would be safer elsewhere? I'd had to show her there were important issues at stake.

"Oh that would be such a shame, Aunty," I said. "They've been in the family so long and they're part of what makes this house a home. We'd miss them terribly."

She'd smiled. "Perhaps you're right."

I was pleased with that. You see Aunty Wendy is very keen on doing the right thing. I'm sure she wanted to keep hold of the old tat but thought that was being selfish. Keeping it for me allowed her to do what she wanted with a clear conscience. It was the same with me living with her in that huge wreck of a house.

"I'm not quite sure it's fair keeping you here dancing attendance on me," she said another time.

"But I like being here." Well, I liked being where I could keep an eye on my inheritance without spending a penny or lifting a finger. Aunty Wendy had a housekeeper, gardener, odd job man and cook. I wasn't so keen on the location. Everyone, it seemed, in the dismal town was related to each other and suffered hereditary distrust. If Aunty Wendy could see my losing the charity money was just an accident, why couldn't they?

"Besides you've been so good to me, I want to offer you what help I can in return," I told her.

"It's nice of you to say that, but I know you young things like your independence and to be around people your own age. I should let you have a job and live in a flat in town."

"No!" I was properly worried. I didn't want a job. I didn't want friends who'd expect me to pay my way and I didn't want a flat I'd have to clean. "That wouldn't be fair at all, would it?"

"It wouldn't?" Aunty Wendy asked.

"No. I'd be taking a job and affordable home from someone who really needed it."

"Oh, I hadn't thought of it like that."

As I arranged a plate of her favourite biscuits and carried our tea in, I guessed her quandary was because she was beginning to see things my way.

It turned out I was wrong, though I didn't find out for a couple of days.

"Jemima dear, I've found the answer to our little problem."

"You have?" I wasn't aware we had a problem, large or small. Aunty Wendy seemed perfectly happy and that suited me. She'd already made it clear that she was leaving everything to me, when she eventually completed the paperwork. I didn't mind waiting while she enjoyed whatever time she had left.

"Yes. I've arranged for you to work for Lord Huntington-Phipps at Huntington Hall."

"But… I…"

"It'll be perfect. You love antiques and historical buildings, don't you?"

No. I loved the idea of cashing them in at the earliest opportunity, but had to nod in agreement.

"You'll be able to stay living here."

That was something.

"The best bit though is that it's a voluntary position."

"Great."

The sarcasm was wasted on her. Still, at least I got her to cough up for a car for me. Nice little sporty number; well worth a few days' work. I had no intention of staying at Huntington Hall any longer than that.

Everything about the job was awful. The house was even more of a wreck than Aunty Wendy's place and had even more junk in it. Everything was roped off or locked up though, so if there had been anything interesting it would be hard to get a good look and impossible to pocket it. The fires weren't lit, the pantry wasn't stocked with lovely food and drink, and all the flowers were plastic. I couldn't even sit in the chairs. I was expected to clean things and learn about them so I could entertain the visiting public. It was demeaning.

"Are you enjoying it?" Aunty Wendy asked when I

returned from my first cold, hard and miserable day.

"To be honest I feel a little uncomfortable. It doesn't seem right to charge people who, through no fault of their own, haven't had the good fortune to live somewhere like that, to come in and look round someone's home." That should make sure she didn't get it into her head to donate her house to the National Trust.

"I am sorry, dear. I don't know what to say. Lord Huntington-Phipps needed help and I thought this would suit you and…" Poor dear looked quite miserable.

"You weren't to know, Aunty. Don't worry, I won't let him down. I'll stay as long as he wants me and that will give me the chance to see if having a job really would suit me."

"If you're sure, Jemima dear."

"Absolutely."

She looked a lot happier. "I'm so pleased to hear you say that. You see I've asked for a report on you… "

"Oh?"

"You always say the kindest things and want to look after me and I worry I'm holding you back. Perhaps I shouldn't have done it though?"

Of course she shouldn't. Nowhere in my plans was there a need for her to think for herself or make decisions without consulting me. "It's fine, really. I'm happy staying here looking after you, but if a second opinion will reassure you then that's fine too." I was positive Lord H-P wouldn't want me around for long and pretty sure he'd report to Aunty Wendy that employment wasn't really for me.

At work the next day I was trying to think of a way to make sure my services were no longer required when I recognised a visitor. He was on his own and looking jumpy, just as he'd been when I, quite literally, bumped into him in a charity shop a few weeks previously. The chap had victim written all over him. I kept him in my sights as I worked out what to do. That didn't take long, then all I had to do was take up position on the half landing and wait.

"Don't touch that!" I yelled across Lord Huntington-Phipps' recently restored smoking room.

As I'd expected, the timid little man, who'd been in no danger of actually making contact with the glazed painting, and in little danger of damaging it if he had, leapt back.

The enormous antique vase he'd stumbled against teetered for a moment. As it rocked time really did seem to stand still, just like people say. For a moment I didn't think it would fall, but it did and shattered with an explosive crash.

"Oh," he whimpered. "Oh my."

I felt my face redden and body judder with the effort of not laughing.

Lord H-P guided everyone out the room and for the first time I saw some point to those silly little bags he made everyone put on their feet before looking round the miserable old house. It stopped that rotten old china scratching their shoes.

"Would you fetch the camera from my office please, Jemima," he said. Lord H-P I mean, not the shy little man. I expect he'd scarpered the minute he got outside. I would of.

"Sure thing." I was back with it in a minute. "A picture for the insurance is it?"

"Yes, that's right."

I took snaps from all angles, making sure to show there was plenty of space round the table on which the vase had stood. "Don't want them refusing to pay up, do we?" I asked him.

"No, I suppose not, though what good the money will do I

don't know. That vase was irreplaceable."

"Don't be daft. For what that was probably worth you can get loads of vases down the High Street and plenty left over for real flowers to go in them too. Nice modern vases won't leak like that old thing would. Though why you worry I don't know. The table it's on is in a right state. Tell you what, we could put it near the fireplace and let that have an accident too and you could get a nice set of pine nesting tables."

"Too?" he queried. "You mean the vase breaking was no accident?"

"Of course not."

As anticipated he realised he probably could manage without my help after all. In fact he didn't even need me to stay and sweep up the mess.

The excitement made me hungry, so I stopped in town for a snack on my way home. The department store was the most expensive place for tea and cakes but they're very good and Aunty had an account set up there.

When I got back I was surprised to hear a man's voice coming from Aunty Wendy's sitting room. I crept up the stairs and listened at the door trying to work out if her visitor was Lord H-P. It wouldn't have suited me at all for him to give his report before he'd had a chance to calm down and I'd given my version of events. I slipped along to Aunty's room and grabbed her heart pills. If things went badly she might be wanting them and then who's she going to believe? The bully of a lord insulting her nearest relative, or that same sweet girl who was administering the treatment she needed?

I heard Aunty say, "That must be Jemima now," so I went in.

Aunty was sat by a roaring fire, holding a paper file. Her visitor, visible only as a silhouette against the low evening light, was looking out over the gardens. He looked like an angel, due partly to the glow around him from the setting sun, but mainly because he so clearly wasn't Lord Huntington-Phipps.

"Jemima dear, come in and say hello to my solicitor, Mr Milde. Although of course you've met him already."

"I have?" I had wanted to certainly. I stepped toward him with my hand extended and charming smile switched on. "Nice to meet you, Mr Milde." As I said his name he turned and I realised Aunty Wendy was right; we had met in a way. Her solicitor was the man who'd broken the vase at Huntington Hall. I felt slightly light-headed.

"Oh, I'm so sorry," the solicitor whispered, stuttering and stumbling over every word. "I've reminded you of that horrible incident. The shock must have been awful for you."

"Well, yes." That response seemed more tactful than, "Actually I planned it and it went beautifully."

"Mr Milde was telling me how seriously you took your job, how protective you were of the treasures and how distraught you were after the accident."

I nodded, wondering where this would go.

"He came straight here to give his report, just as I asked him."

So I'd been wrong in assuming it was H-P who'd been asked to inform her of my suitability for employment. I had to think quickly. "It was a shock, but in a way I'd been expecting it. All those beautiful things on display and at the mercy of the public. I hated seeing people lean on the lovely old wallcoverings, reach out to touch delicate fabrics, get too close too, oh! ... I'm sure Mr Milde meant to be careful, but… "

The solicitor looked like he wanted to run away.

Aunty Wendy shuddered. I was sure she was imagining sticky fingered children handling her ornaments and scuffing their feet on her ancient carpets, while their parents faded paintings with flash photography and knocked ornaments over with their bags. Maybe she also realised I shouldn't be made to mix with such people.

"I've thought about everything you've told me, Jemima dear, and I see you're absolutely right."

I gave a modest nod.

"We can't allow this house to fall into the hands of an organisation that would open it up to the public and we can't allow its treasures to be removed. I know you feel just as I do on these and so many other points. That's why I've had Mr Milde draw up my will this afternoon. "

"Oh." Fantastic!

"Perhaps you would care to see it?" Mr Milde asked, in the same shaky way as he'd spoken before. "After your trauma earlier today it might help set your mind at rest to know your aunt's treasures won't suffer the same fate." He took the file from Aunty and handed it to me.

"Thank you." I read it carefully. Every physical thing of my aunt's was entrusted to me. I was to live in the house, caring for it and its contents. A modest income would be allotted to me to allow me to continue in that role permanently, but would cease were I to leave. The money was to be administered by Mr Milde, who didn't look to me like an overly generous man. Neither the house, nor items in it, could be sold or otherwise disposed of during my lifetime. It had already been witnessed. I was trapped forever.

"This way you can be sure of always living here, just as

you do now," Aunt Wendy said.

"Yes, I see."

"I'll ring for some tea," she said.

"The staff are just going home," I pointed out. There was no mention of them staying on in the will I realised. "I'll go and make it." It seemed I'd have to get used to doing everything.

Down in the kitchen I tipped rat poison into the cup I intended to give Mr Milde. It would be a horribly painful death. I emptied the cup and rinsed it clean; poisoning him wouldn't solve the problem of the will and it would be hard to pass it off as an accident.

At the top of the stairs I paused with the tray in my hands and looked around for inspiration. The family portraits got me thinking. When I showed Mr Milde out, would seeing him near them remind me of the terrible accident he'd caused earlier? I thought it might. The shock would probably make me come over quite faint and clutch at the timid Mr Milde for support. The poor, dear man would, I thought, be so alarmed by this he'd stumble and crash down the stairs, breaking his neck at the bottom. Naturally I'd rush down after him, hoping there was something I could do. In my haste I could kick his dropped briefcase into the open fire where it, and the will it contained, would be quite destroyed by the time the ambulance arrived.

We drank our tea almost in silence, then I said I'd show Mr Milde out. I found myself in a quandary. Would I push him, or would I not?

Stupid of me but I didn't. Maybe Aunty Wendy's niceness had infected me?

"I owe you an apology," he mumbled.

He owed me a lot more than that I reckoned. Without his

interference I'd have got just what I wanted. As it was, it looked like what I'd be getting was closer to what I deserved.

"I'd heard you were no g-good. But you're magnificent."

He was right of course, but did he think I didn't know?

"So forceful. So loyal."

"Are you trying to propose or something?"

He jumped higher than he had at Huntington Hall and landed further from his starting position than he had the first time I'd startled him. When he came down only half his left foot was on the top step. The other made contact with nothing but air.

Just as the vase had done earlier, he seemed to teeter. I really thought I'd have to shove him after all, but finally he fell. Straight down he went. He'd have broken his neck for sure, had not Lord Huntington-Phipps arrived at that moment and caught him. As it was the sensitive little solicitor was out cold.

"Another accident, Jemima?" Lord H-P asked. He placed Mr Milde on a convenient chaise longue.

Slowly I walked down to join them. "What are you doing here?"

As Lord Huntington-Phipps loosened the solicitor's tie and checked his pulse, he explained. He'd decided that I, rather than his insurance company, should pay for the broken vase and had come to say that if I agreed it would be the end of the matter. He told me the sum involved and I calculated it would also be the end of my savings, my shiny new car and any money I could acquire in the foreseeable future.

Mr Milde opened his eyes and started to mumble. Lord Huntington-Phipps bent to listen and spoke to him gently.

Aunty Wendy was making her slow, careful way down the stairs. I didn't have long.

Lord Huntington-Phipps meanwhile was still going. "I trusted you, Jemima. Trust is a privilege. It shouldn't be abused."

He was a fine one to talk about abuse after using me as a slave, then trying to extort money from me. Mr Milde was no better, sneaking around spying on me then drafting my aunt's will so he'd get control of the money.

"What's going on here?" Aunty Wendy asked.

She was different from them. She was the one who'd sorted out that bit of trouble I'd got in after accidentally using other people's credit cards a while back, and who'd provided me with a home.

"This has been a shock for everyone," I said. "Let me fetch some brandy."

Lord H-P accompanied me and watched as I set the decanter and crystal goblets on a silver tray. I picked it up and though my hands shook he didn't try to help me. I set it down again. He watched as I removed the stopper from the decanter and slopped brandy into a glass. Again he offered no assistance. Turning slightly away I took Aunty Wendy's pills from my pocket and tipped some into my hand. I knew they'd slow my racing heart and make me feel calmer. I had no idea how long it would take for Aunty's pills to stop it entirely. I hoped it would happen quite quickly, before anyone had the chance to tell Aunty Wendy the truth. Once I was dead there would be no need for her to be told and she could mourn my death as just one more accident.

Lord H-P grabbed my wrist. "Oh no you don't."

"I don't have an alternative."

"No, you don't. I said you must pay me back and that's exactly what you'll do. My dear cousin Malcolm Milde has just been telling me how much he admires you. You may have noticed he's a little timid?"

There should have been a clever answer to that, but I couldn't think of one.

"He gets taken advantage of because of it. Clients make him take jobs he doesn't want, he's sold advertising and services he doesn't need and nobody pays their bills. That could all stop with you as his assistant."

I saw his point. If you wanted someone with experience of manipulators and cheats who didn't pay their way, I was very well qualified.

"You want me to work for him and give all my wages to you?"

"Until you've paid for the vase. Shouldn't take more than fifteen years."

I returned the pills to the bottle and gulped down a glass of brandy.

"You agree?" he asked.

"Like you say, I have no choice." I carried in the tray, poured brandy for the others and refilled my glass before taking a seat on the chaise longue next to my new employer. My nervous, easy to manipulate employer, who admired me and had Aunty's will in his briefcase.

19 Someone To Talk To

Penny is moving back.

"On the right of you, this time, Cyril. My old flat wasn't available."

"From what I remember, lass, you were always on my right side."

It wasn't much of a joke but she chuckled politely. "I'm glad we'll be neighbours again," she said.

I was glad too. It's nice to have a pretty young neighbour to talk to. I felt guilty about my pleasure. She was back because her marriage was over.

I'm not young or strong enough to help with moving furniture and boxes. I made cups of tea and plenty of toasted cheese for her more able helpers. Her brother drove the van. He'd recruited some chaps who'd done this kind of thing before. I've seen plenty of people get caught out by the stair's sharp turns and metal banisters. Nothing of Penny's got dented or knocked. Nothing physical at any rate. Her heart and spirit were badly bruised, but that happened at her old house, not here.

Penny had never been confident. Now she was positively timid. She went to work; spoke to people there of course. 'Would you like help packing?' and 'Any cash back?' Never really talked to anyone though, just me.

"What about those internet chat rooms, then?" I suggested.

"What good would they be?"

"You wouldn't need to be shy. You just type stuff, no talking. Bloke down the Legion was telling us about it.

Reckons it's great. You never have to give a smart reply straight away. You wait till you think of something good."

"But I don't even have a computer."

"You could buy one second-hand quite cheap."

"I suppose so. I could ask someone at work for advice. It would be nice to have something different to talk about."

"Conversation not up to much?"

"I suppose they are trying to be friendly, but I'm fed up with people asking me why I call myself Mrs Moore when I don't have a wedding ring."

"You still call yourself that?"

"Yes. I hate it."

"Then change it."

"Can you just do that?"

"Why not? What about Miss Less?"

"Penny Less? I don't think so, that's a bit too close to the truth at the moment." She did smile though. "What about Arcade? I might get lucky with that. Or Ms Pinching, that'd stop anyone thinking I was an easy touch."

"Or Chew, because you're so sweet?"

"Whistle, as I'm loud or Penny Farthing because I go round in circles? Perhaps I'll just go back to my maiden name."

"Good idea. And there's a lot of other things you can change too, if you want."

"Like that ex-husband of mine you mean? All I got from my marriage was a pale circle on my finger and dark circles under my eyes."

Her social life involved playing Scrabble with me in the flat, or accompanying me to the Legion for a game of dominoes with the lads. I call them lads because they're younger than me, some of them by as much as twenty years. There's not one of them doesn't draw a state pension.

"You should mix with younger people, make friends."

Penny didn't want to. "I've been hurt enough. I'd rather be lonely, thanks."

She hadn't just lost her husband you see, but her best friend too. That's why she'd divorced him. They'd had an affair, whilst Penny worked extra shifts to pay the mortgage. They live in the house now.

"You don't have to get married or anything. It's just people to talk to, share a joke with."

"I've got you, you're a good friend."

"I'm eighty-nine, have bad breath, a dodgy hip and even dodgier jokes. I'm not what you need."

She said she liked my jokes, but didn't deny the bad breath. Hmm, I'd better ask one of the lads down the Legion about that.

"I'm really too shy. Can you imagine me dressed to kill down the nightclub?"

True enough; Penny was not really a nightclub kind of girl. Her ex-best friend had been apparently. The less said about that the better I figured.

I think she just got the computer to stop me nagging at her. Bought it second-hand at PC Planet down the High Street. 'Our deals are out of this world!' that's what they reckon, not so sure myself. She had a lot of problems with that computer. Different bits of software weren't compatible. I didn't really understand. She told me the computer was sick.

"Not just the computer, lass."

"Cyril, what's wrong?" Frightened, she looked.

"Don't fret. Just meant me hip. I'm having it done next week."

"You never said. Why the rush?"

"No rush. I've known for months. Pretended it wasn't going to happen. I'm just a bit nervous like."

"You listen constantly to my problems, which aren't much really. I should have been helping you."

"Glad you feel like that. You could come with me to the hospital. They said someone could stay with me. Just until they give the injection. I'd rather not wait on me own."

"Of course. And I'll come back afterwards, as soon as they let me."

She was as good as her word. We did crosswords as we waited. Me in my hospital gown and her sat on the bed. Nurses thought she was my daughter. I didn't correct 'em. I'd like the girl to be mine. All she said was, "What's three across, Pops?"

I didn't look up, just touched her hand.

"They'll let me visit more if they think I'm family," she said.

Penny has no relations as far as I can tell.

"Family is how I think of you."

"Can I call you Pop then? Even when the nurses aren't listening?"

I suddenly felt all sentimental. Must have been the effect of the pre-med.

The operation went well. I was given exercises to do and in a few days I could walk more easily than I had for years. There was no pain. Silly thing was I got frightened of stairs. I could walk on the flat as far as I liked. I could pick things off the floor or carry a bag of shopping. I didn't want to climb the stairs though. It felt awkward. Truth is, I was afraid of falling. They got me a new place to live. Ground floor, with a warden to check on us. I liked the idea, some of my friends live there. When I need more help it will be available.

Penny helped me settle in. She brought the plants from my old place. Her chatter cheered me up. She seemed happier, told me about her computer friends. My new place has quizzes and sing-alongs all sorts of things that old boys like me enjoy. I was busy making new friends and it seemed Penny was too.

She visited me often. She came to the little party I had to celebrate the first birthday of my new hip. They like celebrating things here. It doesn't take much for them to get out the sherry and cakes.

"I've got something to celebrate, too."

That's when I noticed the ring.

"Can I bring him to see you, Pops?"

Really nice chap young Andy is. I think this time the 'for better for worse' will have some better in it. He's got a good job too Penny said. He works on the helpdesk at PC Planet.

20 Getting Away

Naomi studied the advert carefully. She couldn't see a catch. The offer was limited to just one date, but that date was perfect. 'Take a car and up to four people to France for £10 plus three more of these vouchers' it invited. Surely Bill couldn't object to that? Naomi had her birthday money from Tony, £50. That should cover the fare and petrol.

If Bill was in a good mood when he returned from his latest business trip, she'd suggest the break would be good for both of them. He worked hard and she understood that travelling for work wasn't the same as going on a holiday.

Naomi's own travel bag was still in good condition. She sighed. When she'd been given it she'd looked forward to travelling. She'd only ever taken it as far as the local maternity unit.

They hadn't gone on honeymoon, buying a house had been more important. Bill had promised to take her the following year. Her passport arrived the day she learnt she was pregnant. Almost nine years and six children later, although Bill frequently travelled for his work, Naomi had still never been abroad. Weeks in the Caribbean were now an impossible dream, but a short trip on their tenth anniversary didn't seem too extravagant. Tony, Bill's brother, would help with the children she was sure. Tony was a solicitor, usually free at weekends and he loved his nieces and nephews. He'd offered to babysit several times, but Bill never thought much of Tony's suggestion he take Naomi out for a meal.

"Waste of money. Naomi's cooking's good enough for

me."

The phone rang, waking the baby. She held the child with one arm and grabbed the receiver.

"Can I speak to Mr Bayley please?"

"Sorry he's not here. I'm Mrs Bayley, can I help?" Naomi offered, although the baby screaming in her ear made it difficult to concentrate.

"I'm so sorry to bother you when you're ill, but it appears Mr Bayley took home a file that's needed urgently."

"I'm not ill."

"Oh sorry, I just assumed that. It must be nice having such an understanding husband. Most men think looking after the children isn't real work. At least yours realises you need a break occasionally."

What was the woman talking about? Bill thought her life was one long break.

"What is it you need?"

After listening to the caller's explanation, Naomi promised that if the missing file was in the house she'd post it first class.

She opened Bill's briefcase. She'd wondered on Sunday why he hadn't taken it. Usually it never left his sight. Something wasn't right. Bill was on a business trip in America. She knew that as she'd spent Saturday evening washing, ironing and packing for him. His company seemed to think he was at home helping her care for the children. Although she couldn't think of one, she was sure there must be a reasonable explanation.

Naomi found the file. She also found the photograph of a young woman and credit card statements showing payments for flights to Europe, hotels, restaurants and jewellers. She could come up with an explanation for these, but it certainly wasn't reasonable. She folded one statement and tucked it into her pocket. She didn't want Bill claiming she was imagining things, like the time he'd claimed to be staying with his mother whilst she recovered from her knee replacement. When Naomi had rung to wish her well, she'd learnt that Tony, not Bill was in attendance. Bill claimed his mother was confused and Naomi hysterical.

She didn't have time to worry about it now. She had to get her two youngest into the buggy, the twins into warm coats and collect the eldest two from school. There was another load of washing to hang out too.

When Bill telephoned, she told him about the call from work.

"That will have been Mavis Rutledge who called, I expect?"

"Yes."

"I told the boss not to hire her. That's the trouble with menopausal women, half the time they can't remember their own name, let alone run an office. Get all emotional if you say anything though."

"I sent the file in."

"You know you're not supposed to touch my briefcase. Commercial in confidence that is. I hope you didn't look at anything you shouldn't have?"

"No, Bill."

His mood when he arrived home later that week didn't encourage her to suggest the trip to France, but she did cut out the second voucher from the local paper.

A fortnight later Bill returned from work very late.

"I've had some bad news. Tony's been in an accident."

"Oh, Bill! No."

"He's not too bad, but I must go to him. Sorry, but I'll be away for our anniversary."

"Would he like to come here?"

"No, he doesn't want to leave the house. It's shaken him up pretty badly."

Naomi hoped Tony would come to stay. She wouldn't mind the extra work, not that there would be much. He didn't leave things all over the house for her to pick up. When she prepared a meal, he thanked her. He sometimes washed up afterwards, persuading the older children to dry and put away. He was kind. He spoke to her, not down to her.

She realised how little contact she'd had with him since Janie, her youngest was born. He'd come to the barbecue Bill had insisted on. At eight months pregnant she'd found the preparations exhausting. She'd just kicked off her shoes, to ease her swollen ankles, when Tony arrived asking if he could help.

"It's it all sorted, come and have a beer," Bill had called.

"Will you be cooking?" Tony asked.

"Can't cook and drink can I?"

"Don't let him keep you barefoot and pregnant forever," Tony had said whilst helping her carry out chairs and cool drinks. Bill hadn't liked that, she remembered.

As Bill left for work the following morning, he warned her he'd be late home. "I have a lot to do, before I go to Tony's."

Naomi started the first washing load of the day and found the credit card receipt she'd kept. She thought of Tony, was he really injured? She rang him.

That afternoon she went through the ritual of gathering her children together, but she didn't bring them home. Instead they all took a bus and went to Bill's office. Naomi wasn't surprised to see him leave at five. He was surprised to see them.

He looked shocked when she said, "Bill, good news. Tony has almost recovered from his accident."

"That's right, Bill," said Tony. "In fact all I need now is a few days away. I've just booked flights to Tenerife. Don't worry, Naomi will take good care of me."

"But what about me and the kids?"

"I've arranged for your mother to look after the children whilst I'm away," Naomi told him. "You'll have to look after yourself."

"For how long? I've got an important meeting next week, I'll need my suit cleaned and ironed."

"Forever, Bill. I think this explains everything." Naomi handed him his credit card statement. On the back, she'd written a note, explaining that although she was going on a break with Tony she would have her own room. She wasn't leaving Bill for Tony, but she would be taking her brother-in-law's advice about divorce proceedings when she returned.

21 Hairy Situation

"Would you like a drink first?" asked the young man who was the cause of Dave's present trouble.

Dave shook his head in answer. He'd be wanting a beer afterwards, but he wouldn't even taste it if he had one now. He could delay no longer, every minute he put off the inevitable, was another minute of awful anticipation.

From across the street, Dave glared at the front of Jean Paul's unisex salon. If anyone other than his wonderful daughter had asked him to go in there, he would have refused without a moment's hesitation. It was bad enough that in a few weeks' time she'd be getting married to this awful boy and moving out of her home, he couldn't disappoint her regarding her wedding plans and he wouldn't leave her with the memory of his silly fear.

Dave hated hairdressers, had done since he was a child. More than hated them. Almost every unpleasant memory he had from his mostly happy childhood was connected with a barber's shop, a salon or simply a person with scissors in their hand and a wish to remove hair.

There had been the pudding basin cuts he'd had when his mum had been ill. Instead of her gently brushing his hair and snipping off the stray ends, his dad had tugged a comb through his untidy thatch, plonked on the basin and trimmed round it as neatly as his big, strong hands would allow. The scissors were tiny, Dave had wriggled and his dad was never a patient man. He did his best. His best hadn't been very neat.

Dave remembered having to sit for hours and hours with

nothing but an out-of-date comic while he waited for hus granny's blue rinse to be dry and her permanent wave to be set. His mates had been at the Saturday matinee while Dave had to sit still and be good.

Even worse was when his beloved terrier, Scruff had become ill. Scruff wouldn't eat, yet his belly got bigger and bigger. The vet had shaved off Scruff's fur, ready to operate, but Scruff had died before the first incision. Now, Dave knew the removal of the hair hadn't been what killed Scruff, but he still couldn't bear to hear the sound of electric clippers.

As soon as he'd been old enough, Dave had refused to allow anyone to cut his hair. He grew it long and kept it tidy in a ponytail. When the ends looked ragged, he snipped them off. These days his ponytail started much further back on his forehead than it used to, but that didn't worry him. Some people probably sniggered behind his back and thought he was having a mid-life crisis, but Dave didn't care. If his ponytail kept him away from the sound of the shears, the smell of ammonia and peroxide, the sting of shampoo in his eyes, then Dave would keep his ponytail. Unfortunately the time had come when he could no longer avoid such horrors.

"Please, Daddy," his daughter had pleaded. "This is very important to me. I want everyone to look the same…"

He'd given in. His love for her was greater than his dislike of a bunch of scissors-wielding sadists. No, stop it, he told himself. They're just people who happen to cut hair for a living. You haven't been near a hairdresser's for years; they won't be the same people. Probably the techniques and chemicals and equipment had changed too in the last forty years.

Dave watched until he was sure no customer was about to approach the desk. No sense in having to spend a moment longer in the place than he needed to. He took a deep breath, looked right and left and crossed over the street.

Pushing open the door, he was immediately engulfed in the hot, damp chemical laden air he remembered. The boring, irritating chatter and the metallic bites of the blades were audible even above the terrifying roar of the dryers and the awesome destructive sound of the electric shears. Dave realised he was allowing his frightened imagination to run away with itself and forced himself to concentrate on the girl perched on a high stool behind the counter.

"I've come about an appointment," he croaked out.

"Certainly, sir. What will it be for?"

"A wedding."

"No, sorry, I meant will you be requiring a cut and blow dry, colouring?"

"No!" Dave almost shouted. "No," he said again, more calmly. "Nothing like that."

"Ah! Just a trim then, or maybe you'd like it done with the shears?"

"No, no. None of you are touching my hair."

Dave backed towards the door. As soon as he stepped away from the counter, his legs seemed to weaken and shake.

"Are you OK, sir?" the girl asked.

"I will be in a minute. Please, just check your diary for the twenty-fifth of next month."

Obligingly, the girl quickly flipped through to the relevant page. "Ah! That wedding. We have the bride, the mother of the bride, the matron of honour and three bridesmaids booked in to have their hair dressed."

"That's right and I've come to pay for it."

Dave swiped his card and punched in his PIN without pausing to glance at the total. This place had enough horrors without adding that.

"Thank you, sir. I understand the bride wishes everyone to have similar styles; will you be requiring a booking for the men in the wedding party?"

"That won't be necessary," Dave said as he collected his receipt.

Thanking his lucky stars that his future son-in-law had the good sense to wear his hair in a nice, neat ponytail Dave crossed over the street to join that admirable young man in a drink.

22 Blue Mondays

Most people look forward to the weekend. Marie didn't; she looked forward to a few stolen hours on Monday afternoons. Weekends were spent with her children and husband. It's not that she didn't love them; she did. She enjoyed being with them but it was very tiring. Her whole life was tiring from when she lit the range in the morning to when she shut up the chickens at night. If it was just hard work she wouldn't have minded. She was fit and healthy; she could cope with work. It was her mind that was tired, her heart, her soul. Everything that was Marie was tired.

Fortunately she was still in touch with a sympathetic friend from her school days. Claire was always ready to listen whenever Marie phoned.

"My life hasn't turned out how I wanted."

"In what way?"

"I didn't expect living out in the country to ever make me feel so isolated and hopeless. I thought a healthy rural life would be best for us and the children."

"Isn't it? A huge garden, fresh air, no traffic jams was your idea of paradise. You were doing so great, making your own bread, producing eggs and vegetables…"

"Oh yes, I loved it when we first came here, but that was before Martin."

"A child with muscular dystrophy is hard work. You do a great job. He has a good life. It's you that needs more."

"He's my son. I love him. I love my other kids too. I can't spare enough time for them."

"It's not easy. Even if like mine, your kids are healthy. Thank God."

"Many of the places the older ones like, I can't take Martin. Activities they enjoy, Martin can only ever watch. I'm too tired to be an enthusiastic mother or a wife."

"That's not good. Your marriage will suffer. You need an escape from the routine."

"Got any suggestions?"

"Ring that agency I told you about."

"I can't do that. I'm a wife, a mother. I have responsibilities."

"You're not the Marie you used to be. You need to cut free from those responsibilities for a while. Go on, live dangerously."

Marie would have argued, expressed doubt about allowing a stranger such an intimate part in her life. She would have said she was concerned about losing her family's trust. She didn't, her conversation was interrupted.

"Mum, I'm hungry, when's tea ready?"

"Must go, I'll call you back."

She didn't.

The cat was sick on Martin, so he was sick too. Whilst she was clearing them up, smoke from the oven activated the fire alarm. Martin screamed.

Her husband came home expecting his evening meal. He found; one son half-dressed and still wet; the other children hungry and upset; the cat retching on the stairs and his wife crying on the kitchen floor.

The following day, once everyone except Martin had left for school or the office, she rang the agency.

"I'm a mother, wife, cook, cleaner, gardener, emotional

counsellor. I want to rediscover the woman I used to be."

"Every woman would sympathise. I know of a man who'll be perfect for you. I guarantee he'll help you forget your problems for a few hours."

Marie wasn't so sure that a happy couple of hours could sort out her life. She didn't think it was worth the guilt over no longer being the perfect wife and mother everyone thought she was. Then she met Devon and was convinced. If anyone could bring back the old Marie, then it was Devon. She didn't have to tell him what she wanted; he knew.

Monday afternoons became an indulgence. She felt like a schoolgirl waiting for a date as she cleared up from lunch. She watched from the kitchen window as he parked outside the house in his shiny yellow car.

"Here I am, are we ready for some fun?" he called whilst bounding up to the front door, his dreadlocks bouncing in time to his long stride. Marie knew her normally observant neighbours must have seen him, but no one mentioned the fact. There was never even the most subtle of comments. No one 'just popped round' during those few precious hours, or told her husband it was nice she had a new friend. They were either more discreet than she gave them credit for, or too shocked to comment.

Marie had fun; every week she tried something different. For two glorious months, she enjoyed a few hours a week when she could just be Marie.

She didn't really feel guilty. She told herself that, hoping she would start believing it. The children were met from school. The house was tidy. Clothes were washed, chicken fed, garden weeded. When her husband returned from work at seven, his family and a hot meal were waiting. Her relationship with her family improved. She remembered what a happy fun person she used to be and reminded them.

One Monday afternoon, Marie heard the phone ringing but didn't get out of the bath to answer it. She put down her paperback and picked up the loofah. Long soaks in scented water were a habit she'd acquired since meeting Devon. Before, a quick shower was all she had time for. Devon ensured her bath was undisturbed. That's why he answered her mother-in-law's call.

"No, Devon! Anyone but her. What did she say?"

"She asked who I was, what I was doing and why."

"And you said?"

"That it was difficult to explain."

"It certainly is. Where did you say I was?"

"In the bath. She's coming round."

"No. What shall I tell her?"

"The truth?"

So she did.

Marie had expected a lecture. Instead she got, "You deserve some fun, you must do what you think's right."

Marie finally stopped feeling guilty. She was so glad she'd taken Claire's advice and spoken to the muscular dystrophy support group.

With the physiotherapy Devon provides, Martin is more comfortable. Marie uses the time when Devon cares for Martin, to go shopping, read or take a relaxing bath. Then she collects her other children from school and shows them the love and attention that had previously been unequally shared with their brother. Mondays give the week a perfect start.

23 Cooking The Books

Mary scraped the gooey pink mess into the dog's bowl. Luckily Splash would eat anything and although it seemed a waste to give all that exotic seafood to a spaniel, it was better than throwing it away. Mary made herself a cup of tea and then reread the recipe she'd copied into her notebook. No; she just couldn't see where she'd gone wrong.

She sighed. It had been a mistake to try and impress her husband with her culinary skills; it never worked. Besides, he loved her for herself, not her abilities in the kitchen. She wouldn't have bothered, except that woman, Mike's mother, had made it all sound so easy.

Mary's mother-in-law is an excellent cook – absolutely no doubt about that. Every time they visit, the entire family are treated to a real feast. It's not just Mary and Mike who are catered for; there are Mike's three brothers and their wives too. Her mother-in-law always managed to produce at least four exquisite courses, without even having the decency to mess up her apron or develop a shiny nose from the steamy heat. Mary and her sisters-in-law joked she must have a cordon bleu chef hidden away somewhere.

The last time there had been a family gathering Mike's mum had served a superb mountain of paella. Every grain of rice had been consumed with immense enjoyment. When everyone had congratulated their hostess she'd insisted that the dish was easy.

"You just throw everything in together and let it simmer."

"I'm sure no one could make it as well as you, Mum," Mike said.

His brothers agreed. They always did and they were always right, or so it seemed to Mary. She could cook reasonably well usually, especially if she stuck to simple dishes, but whenever she tried to reach the high standards set by Mike's mum, she failed miserably. It should have been different this time – how could throwing it all in together and letting it simmer possibly go wrong?

Mary had rung her mother-in-law a few days ago and asked for the recipe. She'd carefully noted down both the ingredients and the method. She'd checked the quantities and the cooking times making sure that every detail was correct. This time she hadn't made the mistake of substituting an apparently similar item when something proved hard to obtain. She had bought every item listed; the correct type of rice, the necessary spices, exactly the right Spanish sausage. Everything had been carefully weighed and each step accurately timed. The resulting paella resembled a glutinous rice soup. She'd cooked it for another twenty minutes hoping the excess liquid would evaporate.

The volume did reduce slightly, but not before the mixture had burnt on the base of the pan. The vegetables disintegrated and the seafood hardened and lost its appetising colour. Mary gave up and ordered a take away.

"Never mind, love, Splash enjoyed it," Mike said.

"I wanted you to enjoy your meal."

"I did. That chicken balti and naan bread were absolutely delicious."

Mary scowled.

"Hey, come here, love," Mike said. "You're not really a bad cook. Except for a few spectacular disasters, you're actually very good."

"I suppose…"

"But it wouldn't matter if you were a rotten cook, I'd still love you."

"Oh, go on, you big softy."

Mike was right, she was getting it all out of proportion.

She remembered that feeling and tried to pass it on to Lucy when her sister-in-law rang up a few days later.

"Help! I've got guests coming to dinner and I'm making Mum's paella and it looks terrible."

"Let me guess, it looks like soup?"

"No, it's really dry and the rice is still hard. My recipe says one pint of water, do you think I should add more?"

"One pint? I used two litres! Maybe it's supposed to be two pints?"

"OK, thanks. I'll try that. Gotta go."

Mary wondered how she could have been so stupid. Mike's mum wouldn't have used litres, why on earth had she written that?

Two days later, Mary visited another sister-in-law, Anne.

"I'll make a cup of tea and if you're feeling brave, you can try a piece of my latest cake," Anne said.

"What do you mean 'brave'? You're a great cook."

"Maybe, but I've made the coffee gateaux our mother-in-law served up at Easter."

"Oooh, lovely."

"It might not be. Something always seems to go wrong when I make any of her recipes."

"That's odd. Let's try the cake."

They each tasted a forkful. The coffee flavour was overpowering.

"Now that's really odd," Mary said. "When I made it, the

flavour was really bland. How much coffee did you use?"

"Two ounces."

"As far as I can remember, I used two teaspoons."

"I bet it was supposed to be two tablespoons. It seems we're not very careful about taking notes."

"Yes, I suppose that must be it," Mary agreed.

When Mary got home, there was an answerphone message to say her mother-in-law had suffered some kind of accident and was in hospital. Mary immediately drove to see her and discovered the poor woman had fallen down her front steps whilst watering her hanging baskets. She'd put her arms out to break her fall and broken both wrists.

"Who's going to look after my garden if I can't lift a watering can? And I won't be able to shop or…"

"Try not to worry too much, Mum," Mary said. "All of us girls will take it in turn to come round and help you." Without checking, she knew the others would agree. They all loved their mother-in-law and were grateful for the help she'd given them as newly-weds setting up their first homes and for the many evenings of baby-sitting and for so many other things.

"Why would you do that? I won't be able to cook or do anything much."

"That's why we'll come; so we can help you. You've done so much for us and now it's our turn to do something for you."

A tear slid down the older woman's face. "I don't deserve you all."

"You rest now and I'll come in tomorrow and see if they'll let me take you home."

At home, she told Mike, "Your mother was really shaken up. I don't think I've ever seen her upset before or in a situation she couldn't cope with."

"I don't think anyone has."

Mary and her three sisters-in-law took it in turns to help their mother-in-law. They tended the garden, cleaned and ironed, shopped and cooked. Between them they didn't make a single bad meal. Instead of cheering up as she recovered from her injuries, Mike's mum became more and more depressed. On the day she had her plaster casts removed the girls met at her house to cook a surprise meal in the hope of raising her spirits. They decided Sandra would make fresh tomato soup; Mary would make the seafood paella, Anne the coffee gateaux and Lucy would cope with the drinks and petit-fours.

Sandra tasted her soup. "Thank goodness for that, the last time I made it was far too salty. Mum's recipe says a teaspoon of salt, but for some reason I used a tablespoon before."

"Oh! That's where I went wrong", Mary said. "Mine was bland, it must have been because I didn't use any salt at all."

When Mary checked their mother-in-law's paella recipe, it called for the two pints of water that she and Lucy had guessed were needed. With the correct quantity of coffee, Anne's gateau was fabulous.

"Cointreau!" Lucy exclaimed. "It was Cointreau, not cochineal that I was supposed to put in my truffles."

"Girls, I was wondering, have any of you ever managed to get right one of Mum's recipes?" Mary asked.

They each confessed they hadn't and began to look through the recipe books. After a few checks, Mary said, "What are the chances of us each getting one item wrong in every single recipe?"

"I was wondering that myself," Sandra said.

"If you mean what I think you mean, Mum's been sabotaging our cookery," Lucy said.

"She wouldn't," Anne said. "She's far too nice for that."

"Well, there's something going on and I'm going to find out what it is," Mary said.

When Mike and his brothers arrived with their mother, Mary sent the men to sit in the garden and have a pre-dinner drink.

"Mum, can you come into the kitchen a minute?"

Mum followed her in and looked around at the almost ready meal. Tears rolled down her face.

"I'm so sorry," she sobbed. "You're all such dear girls and I've been horrible to you."

"It really was deliberate then?" Anne asked. "I don't understand why you'd do it."

"It's so stupid. I did it because I wanted to be liked and now you all hate me and so will my boys when you tell them."

"We don't hate you, Mum," Anne said.

"And your boys never will," Sandra assured her. "Even if we told them, which we won't, they still wouldn't hate you."

"No, we won't tell them," Mary said. "But we do want you to tell us."

"It started when Mike met you, Mary," her mother-in-law said. "His other girlfriends hadn't been much good, but I could see you were different. At first I was happy for him, but then I worried he'd love you more than me."

"Oh. I can understand that, because I thought he'd never love me as much as he loved you."

The older woman patted Mary's hand. "He loves you very much, my dear." She looked round at the girls. "All my boys met lovely women and fell in love. I thought I'd lose them all. I did what I could to still be useful to them and to you, hoping I'd still be needed."

"You've always been brilliant," Anne said. "Our lives would all have been harder without you."

"It's not just the things you've done though, Mum," Mary said. "We love you too. Sorry that I've never said it."

The others all nodded and said they loved her.

"I know you do, girls. I've realised that these last few weeks when you've all been so good to me. Your children are too old to need a babysitter now and you… well, I knew you were being nice to me, not just getting me well enough to help you. That should have made me happy. It would have except I felt so bad about giving you the wrong recipes."

"I still don't understand why you did," Lucy said.

"Because you're all so capable. I wanted to be better than you at something and for my boys to still think I'm the best cook. It was stupid…"

"What's going on in there?" Mike called as he pushed open the kitchen door.

"You can't come in, Mike," Mary said, ushering him back out. "We've had a slight disaster with the meal; nothing that Mum can't sort out though, so we'll be serving it up in just a couple of minutes."

"OK, we'll wait in the dining room."

"That paella looks done, take it off the heat, Mary," Mum said. "Sarah love, there's some fresh basil in the greenhouse, that would make a good garnish for the soup and … thank you, all of you."

"That was a wonderful meal," Mike said an hour later. "I don't know how you turned the girl's disaster into such a triumph, Mum."

"No one cooks like Mum," Mary said.

The boys all agreed.

"That soon won't be true," their mum said. "I've decided to share my secret with my lovely daughters-in-law."

The next time Mary cooked paella, it was very nearly as good as the one Mike's mum rescued the day she had the casts taken off her wrists.

24 Last Shot

I opened the post; bill, bill, final reminder, bill, cheque. This last one was mine, returned due to insufficient funds.

I stared at the graduation photograph on the office wall. My own face looked back; young and confident. The camera never lies; but it rarely shows the whole picture and can't predict the future.

Instead of using my education and skills to create, I'd gone after a quick buck and used them to destroy. I'd done things I shouldn't and was despised even by those in my own despicable trade. The situation was desperate. I needed money and needed it quickly.

The phone startled me. It had been so quiet recently I thought I'd been cut off. Without hope, I lifted the receiver and asked how I could help.

"I want you to get rid of my husband," the woman said.

"Pardon?" I'd heard, I just didn't believe it.

"My husband; I want you to get rid of him."

"I don't do that kind of thing," I lied.

"Why not?"

"I'm a reputable…"

"I'll pay well and I know you need the money," she interrupted.

"How?" I could have kicked myself; I'd admitted she was right.

"I asked another chap, he didn't want the job, but gave me your number. Said you'd do it."

Who could that be? Who would know? I didn't think it was common knowledge. You don't put 'removal expert' on your business card unless you're referring to furniture or rats. Come to think of it, I have dealt with some rats in my time, but that's not the point. There are rules against getting rid of people just because they're inconvenient.

The woman didn't seem to have heard of any rules. She promised a large fee if I'd do the job right away. Before I knew it, I'd agreed she could come round to discuss her requirements. Perhaps she didn't want me to get rid of him completely, I tried to kid myself.

In less than an hour she handed me the pictures. Wedding photos; recent. Things must have gone badly wrong.

"I want him permanently out of my life. Do you understand?"

Reluctantly, I nodded. I understood what she wanted, but not why. He looked like an ordinary enough bloke, not someone who deserved to be… erased.

She showed me other pictures; him laughing at a child who'd fallen over, him drunk, him with a redhead. I could see she had her reasons for wanting him gone. That didn't mean it was OK for me to eliminate the chap though.

She took more photographs from her bag. I looked at the pile of money she placed on my desk. She was right, I decided; he had to go. I agreed to do the job.

She paid me half the money. I was to ring when the job was done. She'd pay the rest then.

The task didn't take long. I called to explain.

"I don't want to know how, just show me it's done," she insisted.

I showed her the proof. She paid.

Now I have to tell someone what I did.

I was once a respectable photo-journalist, but I became a member of the celebrity hounding paparazzi. If I couldn't get the photos I wanted, I faked them. It paid well, until I was found out. Now, in a final attempt at a respectable job, I've opened a photographic studio. I'm still faking it though. I've just digitally altered the wedding photos of a wronged woman's daughter to remove the father of the bride.

25 The Painting

"Did you remember that Mum's bringing the painting when she comes for lunch?" Jeremy said.

"I'm hardly likely to forget, am I? Becky answered.

"No, sorry. It's just, you know what she's like…"

"Don't worry. I'm sure it'll be fine."

Even without the added complication of the painting, Angela, Jeremy's mother, wasn't an easy guest. There was her insistence on proper British food for one thing; Angela was obsessive. Becky tried to buy local, ethically produced food. She avoided battery produced eggs and potatoes flown half way round the world, but sometimes she didn't have time to check every label and occasionally, as a treat in winter, she bought imported fruit.

Angela considered such lapses indicated a person unworthy of the painting. Becky made a mental note to allow an extra hour for the shopping and ensure there were no labels that could possibly offend Angela.

The food issue didn't really bother Becky. The smoking did. She hated the smell of cigarettes that lingered long after Angela had gone. She hated that she and Jeremy inhaled second-hand smoke. Most of all, she hated the harm she knew it was doing to Angela's already delicate health.

"Jeremy, I really think we should ask your mum not to smoke, now that we've moved."

"She won't like it."

"I know, but we don't like her smoking and the fewer cigarettes she has the better it will be for her."

"I suppose."

"I put up with it before, because she'd smoked in the old house before I moved in, but it's different now. This is our home and neither of us like people smoking in it; I don't see why we should have to put up with it. Do you?"

"I don't want a scene when she turns up with the painting. You know how she is …"

Becky did; the painting had been the main topic of family conversation and disagreement for months, possibly for years.

"I'll ring up and tell her that we've decided this house will be smoke free then it won't be a shock for her. I'll explain that we don't want nicotine staining our nice new paintwork or the smell soaking into our soft furnishings, I think she'll understand that. It's no good mentioning her health, she just doesn't listen."

"You're right. Actually, it's a very good idea. As she's leaving the painting here for a couple of weeks she should be pleased we take such good care of things. She'll know we'll take proper care of it," Jeremy said.

"We will, but I still don't understand why she doesn't just leave it at home. It'd be insured there."

"It'll be covered by her insurance here too. She's got it covered for when she loans it out."

"It'd still be covered if she left it though, and she wouldn't have to worry about it getting damaged on the way and best of all, we wouldn't have to look at it."

"Becky!"

"Sorry, but whilst we're being honest here I might as well admit I think it's ugly."

"Yes. It is; but that's not the point."

"Why isn't it? As far as I can see the rotten thing is

nothing more than a worry to Angela and the rest of us. She's always lending it to galleries and getting valuations and falling out with people over it."

Just for a moment, Becky wondered if Angela would prefer the insurance money to the painting. She shook her head; that's how she'd feel, but it was different for Angela. The painting had always been important to her husband's family; it had belonged to them for five generations. The concern was never for the painting itself, but about who would inherit it. For some time it had been assumed Julia would as she was the eldest and also an expert on antiques. That had seemed fair to Jeremy and his younger sister Janie. However, Julia had upset the peace, and her mother, by answering a simple question with honesty.

"I'm thinking of taking a holiday," Angela had told her family. "As you know, the doctor said it would be good for my health. Where do you suggest I go?"

"I suggest you don't worry about the holiday so much and instead listen to his other advice and give up smoking. That's the only thing that's really going to do you any good."

"Thank you for your opinion, Julia," Angela had said coldly.

"It's not just my opinion; it's what the doctor said. All your fussing about healthy food and warm climates is just your way of avoiding the issue."

Soon after that, Angela had decided that Julia was not a sufficiently sensitive person to care for the painting. When she'd heard that Jeremy and Becky were buying a new house, she'd insisted on coming for the final viewing.

"Oh, yes. This is very suitable," she'd said. "An elegant home that will be the perfect setting for the painting."

They'd thought then they were bound to inherit it. That

was until Janie's husband had been voted mayor. Angela had managed to drop the phrase 'my son-in-law the mayor' into forty-three conversations before she'd visited to congratulate him. Janie had been so busy with the aftermath of his campaign that she hadn't prepared for her mother's visit and served shop bought cake. The cake had been neither organic, nor British; it hadn't even been Fairtrade. Such philistines clearly did not deserve the painting.

Angela had rung Becky to ask if she would look after the painting whilst she went on her holiday.

"Of course, if you're worried about it."

"I am and I know you'll take proper care of it."

"Of course we will."

"I thought I could drop it off on my way to the airport."

"Then please come for lunch first. I could do a proper Sunday roast that would set you up for the flight."

"You're a good girl, Becky, to take such good care of me and the painting."

That had been a week previously. Since then, Jeremy had been fretting about the visit. He worried how well his mother would accept the new smoking ban and he worried about the painting.

"Have you thought where we'll put it?" he asked.

"The cupboard under the stairs?" Becky suggested.

"We can't!"

"Of course we can. It'll be perfectly safe there."

"That's not the point."

"Oh yes it is. You hate the painting, I hate the painting. It's our house; we don't have to hang it on our walls if we don't want to."

For a moment, he looked as though he'd disagree with her,

but then he nodded. "What will you tell Mum?"

"We'll tell her that we're quite happy to take care of it for her, just as we said we would, but we don't wish to hang it up."

"She'll think we don't like it."

"She'll be right," Becky said.

"But…"

"She'll leave it to someone else?"

"Well, yes."

"So what if she does? I know it's valuable."

"Very valuable," Jeremy corrected.

"Right. But that's no good unless we sell it."

"We couldn't. It's been in the family for years, Mum will probably put some condition in her will."

"So it won't do us any good. We'll just have to increase the insurance and look at the great ugly thing."

"You're right, Becky. I don't really want it. I never did, I suppose I've just got used to the constant discussion about who should have it and never stopped to consider who wanted it."

"So we're agreed, we'll tell her not to leave it to us?"

Jeremy nodded.

"Good, which means we can stop sucking up to her and stop rowing with your sisters?"

"We don't! …No, you're right we do, or did." He hugged Becky. "I've been silly over this, haven't I? I'm going to ring Julia and Janie and let them know too. Maybe they can sort it out between them and in future we'll avoid a mini family feud every time Mum changes her mind about who's going to get it."

Angela arrived for lunch and waited on the driveway for Jeremy to come out and collect the painting.

"Careful of the car," she said as he manoeuvred the well wrapped package from the back of her Range Rover and took it inside.

"Becky darling, how lovely to see you." Angela pecked her daughter-in-law on the cheek.

"I got your answerphone message, dear, but I'm afraid it made no sense."

"It's quite simple, Mum; we don't want you to smoke in our new house."

"But…" Angela tried to speak.

Becky didn't give her the chance. "We don't want the house smelling of smoke and we don't want to breathe it in ourselves, but mostly, we're worried about you."

"Well, I…"

"The doctor told you that you're just making things worse for yourself and we've decided not to assist you smoke yourself to an early grave."

"If I…"

"And don't think you can threaten me with not leaving the painting to us. We don't want it."

"You don't?"

"No, Mum, we don't," Jeremy spoke for the first time since Angela's arrival.

"Well, then, you'd better put it back into the car."

"Don't be silly, Angela. We said we'd look after it whilst you're away and we will. You can collect it after your holiday and leave it to whoever you wish. Now come in and have your lunch; I've got some organic asparagus for starters that was grown just down the road."

Jeremy headed for the dining room.

Angela didn't move from the hallway. "I don't think I am hungry."

"That's up to you, but you haven't time to take the painting home and still catch your flight. We might not want it, but we will take care of it. I promise." Becky went into the kitchen and put pans of water to heat for the vegetables.

Angela followed her and looked around at the prepared locally grown vegetables, the organic wine and the crystal bowl of trifle on the side.

"The beef was produced by the farm that backs onto our estate and the carrots and potatoes were grown by our neighbour on his allotment. Even the cream for the trifle is local and organic."

"I don't understand why you've gone to so much trouble," Angela said.

"Because it's what you like. I want you to be happy. I want you to be healthy too, that's why I'm not changing my mind about the smoking."

"But you don't want the painting…"

"No, I never did." Becky took the meat from the oven and put it on the carving board. She put the asparagus in the steamer and stirred the gravy all without looking at her mother-in-law. She thought she heard Jeremy's footsteps, but he didn't appear.

Becky put the plates to warm, removed the herb butter from the fridge and began stirring the gravy again.

"Neither did I," Angela said softly.

"Pardon?" Becky stopped stirring.

"I never wanted the painting either. That's how I ended up with it."

"I don't understand."

"It belonged to my husband's aunt."

Becky nodded; she knew that part of the story.

"Everyone in the family sucked up to her, because they wanted her to leave it to them. She told me owning it was a curse in some ways, because she never knew if people really cared for her or just hoped to inherit a valuable object. She knew I didn't like it, so she knew my affection for her was genuine; just like yours and Jeremy's is for me."

Jeremy came into the kitchen and put his arm around her. "It is, Mum," he said. "But still don't leave it to us."

"What am I going to do with it then? I've already told both your sisters they can't have it."

"Why?"

"I rang them when I got your message, Becky; about not smoking. They both told me that you were right. I guessed they'd put you up to it and said they could forget about the painting. Guess what they said?"

"They don't want it either?"

"That's right. Oh well, I'll have a think about it whilst I'm away."

A fortnight later, Angela returned and asked all of her family to visit. She informed them that she'd decided to sell the painting.

"I'm going to divide the money into four. Each of my children's families will get a quarter and I'm going to spend the rest of it myself."

"That's great, Mum," Jeremy said.

"Good plan," Julia agreed.

"Brilliant!" Janie added.

"I'm glad you approve," Angela said and smiled. She

appeared to be waiting for something.

"Have you decided what you'll spend your share on?" Becky asked.

"I have. I'm booking myself into a health farm. I've found one that only serves local organic food and it specialises in helping people quit smoking."

Thank you for reading this book. I hope you enjoyed it. If you did, I'd really appreciate it if you could leave a short review on Amazon and/or Goodreads.

To learn more about my writing life, hear about new releases and get a free exclusive ebook, sign up to my newsletter – subscribepage.io/ItLSNa or you can find the link on my website patsycollins.co.uk

<u>More books by Patsy Collins</u>

Novels

Firestarter
Escape To The Country
A Year And A Day
Paint Me A Picture
Leave Nothing But Footprints
Acting Like A Killer

Little Mallow cosy mystery series

Disguised Murder and Community Spirit in Little Mallow
Dependable Friends and Deceitful Neighbours
in Little Mallow
Deadly Words and Innocent Gossip in Little Mallow

Non-fiction

From Story Idea To Reader
(co-written with Rosemary J. Kind)

A Year Of Ideas:
365 sets of writing prompts and exercises

Short story collections

Over The Garden Fence
Up The Garden Path
Through The Garden Gate
In The Garden Air
Beyond The Garden Wall

Can't Choose Your Family
Keep It In The Family
Family Feeling
Happy Families

All That Love Stuff
With Love And Kisses
Lots Of Love
Love Is The Answer

Slightly Spooky Stories I
Slightly Spooky Stories II

Slightly Spooky Stories III
Slightly Spooky Stories IV
Slightly Spooky Stories V

Just A Job
Perfect Timing
A Way With Words
Dressed To Impress
Coffee & Cake
Not A Drop To Drink
Criminal Intent
Crime In Mind
Making A Move
Days To Remember
A Clean Bill Of Health
Your Good Health